The Children of Green Knowe

Lucy Boston was born in Southport, Lancashire in 1892. She was one of six children and in later years she was to rebel strongly against her extremely strict Methodist up-bringing. During the First World War she left Somerville College, Oxford after a couple of terms to train as a nurse and was posted to France. She married an English officer from the Flying Corps, but later divorced him and began a new life when she bought the Manor House at Hemingford Grey. She fully restored the house which dates back to around 1130 and created a spectacular garden. She was over sixty when she started writing, and *The Children of Green Knowe* and all her subsequent Green Knowe stories were inspired by the house she loved so much. Lucy Boston died in 1990.

After you have finished reading *The Children of Green Knowe* you may be interested in reading the Afterword by Jill Paton Walsh on page 153.

Also by Lucy Boston

THE CHIMNEYS OF GREEN KNOWE
AN ENEMY AT GREEN KNOWE
THE RIVER AT GREEN KNOWE
THE STONES OF GREEN KNOWE
A STRANGER AT GREEN KNOWE

THE SEA EGG

For younger readers

THE CASTLE OF YEW

LUCY M. BOSTON

The Children of Green Knowe

ILLUSTRATED BY PETER BOSTON

PUFFIN BOOKS

To My Son

PUFFIN BOOKS

Published by the Penguin Group
Penguin Books Ltd, 27 Wrights Lane, London w8 5tz, England
Penguin Books USA Inc., 375 Hudson Street, New York, New York 10014, USA
Penguin Books Australia Ltd, Ringwood, Victoria, Australia
Penguin Books Canada Ltd, 10 Alcorn Avenue, Toronto, Ontario, Canada m4v 3b2
Penguin Books (NZ) Ltd, 182–190 Wairau Road, Auckland 10, New Zealand

Penguin Books Ltd, Registered Offices: Harmondsworth, Middlesex, England

First published by Faber and Faber Ltd 1954
Published in Puffin Books 1975
Published in this edition 1994
1 3 5 7 9 10 8 6 4 2

Copyright 1954 by L. M. Boston
Illustrations copyright © Peter Boston, 1994
Afterword copyright © Jill Paton Walsh, 1994

Typeset by Datix International Limited, Bungay, Suffolk
Filmset in 12/15 pt Monophoto Bembo
Printed in England by Clays Ltd, St Ives plc

Except in the United States of America, this book is sold subject
to the condition that it shall not, by way of trade or otherwise, be lent,
re-sold, hired out, or otherwise circulated without the publisher's
prior consent in any form of binding or cover other than that in
which it is published and without a similar condition including this
condition being imposed on the subsequent purchaser

A little boy was sitting in the corner of a railway carriage looking out at the rain, which was splashing against the windows and blotching downward in an ugly, dirty way. He was not the only person in the carriage, but the others were strangers to him. He was alone as usual. There were two women opposite him, a fat one and a thin one, and they talked without stopping, smacking their lips in between sentences and seeming to enjoy what they said as much as if it were something to eat. They were knitting all the time, and whenever the train stopped the click-clack of their needles was loud and clear like two clocks. It was a stopping train – more stop than go – and it had been crawling along through flat flooded country for a long time. Everywhere there was water – not sea or rivers or lakes, but just senseless flood water with the rain splashing into it. Sometimes the railway lines were covered by it, and then the train-noise was quite different, softer than a boat.

'I wish it was *the* Flood,' thought the boy, 'and that I was going to the Ark. That would be fun! Like the circus. Perhaps Noah had a whip and made all the animals go round and round for exercise. What a noise there would be, with the lions roaring, elephants trumpeting, pigs squealing, donkeys braying, horses whinnying, bulls bellowing, and cocks and hens always thinking they were going to be trodden on but unable to fly up on to the roof where all the other birds were singing, screaming, twittering, squawking and cooing. What must it have sounded like, coming along on the tide? And did Mrs Noah just knit, knit and take no notice?'

The two women opposite him were getting ready for the next station. They packed up their knitting and collected their parcels and then sat staring at the little boy. He had a thin face and very large eyes; he looked patient and rather sad. They seemed to notice him for the first time.

'What's your name, son?' asked the fat woman suddenly. 'I've never seen you on this train before.' This was always a question he dreaded. Was he to say his unexpected real name or his silly pet names?

'Toseland,' he said.

'Toseland! That's a real old-fashioned name in these parts. There's Fen Toseland, and Toseland St Agnes and Toseland Gunning. What's your Christian name?'

'That is it – Toseland.'

'Do your mum and dad live round here, son?'

'No, they live in Burma.'

'Fancy that now! That's a long way away. Where are you going, then?'

'I don't know. That is, I'm going to my great-grandmother Oldknow at Green Noah. The station is Penny Soaky.'

'That's the next station after this. We get out here. Don't forget – the next station. And make sure there's some dry land before you get out of the train. The floods are bad there. Bye-bye, cheerio.'

They got out, shouting and joking with the porters and kissing the people who had come to meet them. They started off into the hissing rain as if they loved it. Toseland heard the fat woman's loud voice saying, 'Oh, I don't mind this. I like it, it's our home-rain, not like that dirty London water.'

The train jogged on again and now Toseland was quite alone. He wished he had a family like other people – brothers and sisters, even if his father were away. His mother was dead. He had a stepmother but he hardly knew her and was miserably shy of her. He had been at a boarding-school, and for the last holidays he had been left behind to stay with the head mistress, Miss Spudd, and her old father. They meant to be kind to him, but they never spoke to him without saying 'dear'. It was 'Finish up your porridge, dear, we don't want you to get thin,' or 'Put on your coat, dear, we don't want you to catch cold,' or 'Get ready for church, dear, we don't want you to grow up a heathen.' And every day after breakfast, 'Run along to your room, dear, we want to read the papers.'

But now his great-grandmother Oldknow had written that he was to come and live with her. He had never seen her, but she was his own great-grandmother, and that was something. Of course she would be very old. He thought of some old people he had seen who were so old that it frightened him. He wondered if she would be frighteningly old. He began to feel afraid already, and to shake it off he thought about Green Noah and Penny Soaky. What queer names! Green Noah was pure mystery, but Penny Soaky was friendly like a joke.

Suddenly the train stopped, and the porters were shouting 'Penny Soaky! Penny Soaky!' Toseland had no sooner got the door open than a man wearing a taxi-driver's hat came along calling:

'Anybody here for Green Noah? Are you Master Toseland for Green Noah?'

'Oh yes, please. It's me.'

'This your luggage? Two more in the van? You stand here out of the rain while I get it.'

There were a few houses to be seen on one side of the line, and on the other nothing but flooded fields with hedges standing in the water.

'Come along,' said the taxi-man. 'I've put all your luggage in the car. It'll be dark before we get there and we've got to go through a lot of water.'

'Is it deep?'

'Not so deep, I hope, that we can't get through.'

'If it rains forty days and forty nights will it be a real flood?'

'Sure enough it would.'

Toseland sat by the driver and they set off. The windscreen wipers made two clear fans on the windscreen through which he could see the road half covered with water, with ditches brimming on either side. When they came near the bridge that crossed the river, the road disappeared under water altogether and they seemed to drive into the side of the river with a great splash that flew up against the windows; but it was only a few inches deep and then they reached the humpbacked bridge and went up and over it, and down again into deeper water on the other side. This time they drove very carefully like bathers walking out into cold water. The car crept along making wide ripples.

'We don't want to stick here,' said the driver, 'this car don't float.'

They came safely through that side too, and now the headlights were turned on, for it was growing dark, and Toseland could see nothing but rain and dazzle.

'Is it far?' he asked.

'Not very, but we have to go a long way round to get past the floods. Green Noah stands almost in the middle of it now, because the river runs alongside the garden. Once you get there you won't be able to get out again till the flood goes down.'

'How will I get in, then?'

'Can you swim?'

'Yes, I did twenty strokes last summer. Will that be enough?'

'You'll have to do better than that. Perhaps if you felt yourself sinking you could manage a few more?'

'But it's quite dark. How will I know where to swim to?'

The driver laughed. 'Don't you worry. Mrs Oldknow will never let you drown. She'll see you get there all right. Now here we are. At least, I can't go any further.' Toseland pushed the car door open and looked out. It had stopped raining. The car was standing in a lane of shallow water that stretched out into the dark in front and behind. The driver was wearing Wellington boots, and he got out and paddled round the car. Toseland was afraid that he would be left now to go on as best he could by himself. He did not like to show that he was afraid, so he tried another way of finding out.

'If I am going to swim,' he said, 'what will you do with my luggage?'

'You haven't got no gum boots, have you?' said the driver. 'Come on, get on my shoulders and we'll have a look round to see if anyone's coming to meet you.' Toseland climbed on to his shoulders and they set off, but almost at once they heard the sound of oars, and a lantern came round the corner of the lane rocking on the bows of a rowing boat. A man called out, 'Is that Master Toseland?' The driver shouted back, 'Is that Mr Boggis?' but Toseland was speechless with relief and delight.

'Good evening, Master Toseland,' said Mr Boggis, holding up the lantern to look at him, while Toseland looked too, and saw a nice old cherry-red face with bright blue eyes. 'Pleased to meet you. I knew your mother when she was your size. I bet you were wondering how you were going to get home?' It was nice to hear somebody talking about 'home' in that way. Toseland felt much happier, and now he knew that the driver had been teasing him, so he grinned and said: 'I was going to swim.'

The boat was moored to somebody's garden gate while the two men put the trunk and tuck-box into it.

'You'll be all right now,' said the taxi-man. 'Good night to you both.'

'Good night, and thank you,' said Toseland.

Mr Boggis handed him the lantern and told him to kneel up in the bows with it and shout if they were likely to bump into anything. They rowed round two corners in the road and then in at a big white gate. Toseland waved the lantern about and saw trees and bushes standing in the water, and presently the boat was rocked by quite a strong current and the reflection of the lantern streamed away in elastic jigsaw shapes and made gold rings round the tree trunks. At last they came to a still pool reaching to the steps of the house, and the keel of the boat grated on gravel. The windows were all lit up, but it was too dark to see what kind of a house it was, only that it was high and narrow like a tower.

'Come along in,' said Mr Boggis. 'I'll show you in. I'd like to see Mrs Oldknow's face when she sees you.'

The entrance hall was a strange place. As they stepped in, a similar door opened at the far end of the house and another man and boy entered there. Then Toseland saw that it was only themselves in a big mirror. The walls round him were partly rough stone and partly plaster, but hung all over with mirrors and pictures and china. There were three big old mirrors all reflecting each other so that at first Toseland was puzzled to find what was real, and which door one could go through straight, the way one wanted to, not sideways somewhere else. He almost wondered which was really himself.

There were vases everywhere filled with queer flowers — branches of dry winter twigs out of which little tassels and rosettes of flower petals were bursting, some yellow, some white, some purple. They had an exciting smell, almost like something to eat, and they looked as if they had been produced by magic, as if someone had said 'Abracadabra! Let these sticks burst into flower.' 'What if my great-grandmother is a witch!' he thought. Above the vases, wherever there was a beam or an odd corner or a door-post out of which they could, as it were, grow, there were children carved in dark oak, leaning out over the flowers. Most of them had wings, one had a real bird's nest on its head, and all of them had such round polished cheeks they seemed to be laughing and welcoming him.

While he was looking round him, Boggis had taken his coat and cap from him and hung them up. 'Your great-grandmother will be in here,' he said, and led him to a little old stone doorway such as you might find in a belfry. He knocked on the door. 'Come in,' said a clear voice. Boggis gave Toseland a shove, and he found himself inside.

The room seemed to be the ground floor of a castle, much like the ruined castles that he had explored on school picnics, only this was not a ruin. It looked as if it never possibly could be. Its thick stone walls were strong, warm and lively. It was furnished with comfortable polished old-fashioned things as though living in castles was quite ordinary. Toseland stood just inside the door and felt it must be a dream.

His great-grandmother was sitting by a huge open fireplace where logs and peat were burning. The room smelled of woods and wood-smoke. He forgot about her being frighteningly old. She had short silver curls and her face had so many wrinkles it looked as if someone had been trying to draw her for a very long time and every line put in had made the face more like her. She was wearing a soft dress of folded velvet that was as black as a hole in darkness. The room was full of candles in glass candlesticks, and there was candlelight in her ring when she held out her hand to him.

'So you've come back!' she said, smiling, as he came

forward, and he found himself leaning against her shoulder as if he knew her quite well.

'Why do you say "come back"?' he asked, not at all shy.

'I wondered whose face it would be of all the faces I knew,' she said. 'They always come back. You are like another Toseland, your grandfather. What a good thing you have the right name, because I should always be calling you Tolly anyway. I used to call him Tolly. Have you got a pet name? I'm sure they don't call you Toseland at school.'

'No, I get called Towser.'

'And at home?'

'My stepmother calls me Toto, but I hate it. It's worse than Towser.'

'I think I agree with you. Here we are all used to Toseland, it's the family name and doesn't seem queer to us. So you shan't be Toto here. Do you mind Tolly?'

'I like it. It's what my mother used to call me. What shall I call you?'

'Granny,' she said. 'What does one generation more or less matter? I'm glad you have come. It will seem lovely to me. How many years of you have I wasted?'

'Seven,' said Tolly, watching the flames tugging loose from the logs and leaping up the black chimney. They reminded him of bonfire flames wrestling and tearing and whistling in the sky on the fifth of November. Those had been frightening, but these were wonderful.

'Are these our flames?' he asked. 'I mean, are they our own?'

'The blue ones arc yours and the orange ones are mine.'

'And the candle-flames?'

'All yours.'

Tolly hesitated, then asked in a very little voice because he hardly dared, 'Is it my house – I mean, partly?'

'Of course it is – partly, as you say. Well, now that you are here what shall we do first? Are you hungry?'

She rose and, standing, looked much older. Her figure was bent and shrunken, her face no higher than Tolly's own. The folds of her dress seemed both to weigh her down and hold her up. She brought a tray that was laid ready for him on the sideboard, and put it on a low table in front of the fire. There were egg sandwiches and chicken sandwiches and iced orange cake and jelly and chocolate finger biscuits. Toseland ate happily and tried not to make crumbs.

'I came in a boat with a lantern,' he said. 'I played the house was Noah's Ark.'

'Oh, the Ark! So you played it was the Ark.'

'Yes. Do you think Noah had a whip like a circus man and made the animals run round and round for exercise?'

'Yes. And Ham juggled with clubs and plates to pass the time away, and Shem and Japhet were clowns and tried to make Mrs Noah laugh. But she never did, because if she had done, all her buttons would have burst off. She was done up very tight.'

At that moment the fire went *pop!* and shot a piece of wood out into the room. *Pop!* again.

'Buttons! Who said buttons? Poor Mrs Noah.' Tolly chased the sparks and trod on them to put them out.

'Why do you live in a castle?' he said, looking round.

'Why not? Castles were meant to live in.'

'I thought that was only in fairy-tales. Is it a real castle?'

'Of course.'

'I mean, do things happen in it, like the castles in books?'

'Oh, yes, things happen in it.'

'What sort of things?'

'Wait and see! I'm waiting too, to see what happens now that you are here. Something will, I'm sure. Tomorrow you can explore the inside of the house up and down, and learn your way about and to feel at home in it, because you won't be able to go outside until the floods go down. And now you must come and see your own room, and you must go to bed early tonight.'

She led him up winding stairs and through a high, arched room like a knight's hall, that she called the Music Room, and up more stairs to the very top of the house. Here there was a room under the roof, with a ceiling the shape of the roof and all the beams showing. It was a long room with a triangle of wall at each end and no walls at the sides, because the sloping ceiling came down to the floor, like a tent. There were windows on three sides, and a little low wooden bed in the middle covered with a patchwork quilt, as unlike a school bed as anything could be. There was a low table, a chest of drawers and lots of smooth, polished, empty floor. At one side there was a beautiful old rocking-horse – not a 'safety' rocking-horse hanging on iron swings from a centre shaft, but a horse whose legs were stretched to full gallop, fixed to long rockers so that it could, if you rode it violently, both rear and kick. On the other side was a doll's house. By the bed was a wooden box painted vermilion with bright patterns all over it, and next to it all Tolly's luggage piled up, making the room look really his. A wicker birdcage hung from one of the beams. On the only side that had no window there hung a big mirror reflecting all the rest – the rafters, the wicker cage, the rocking-horse, the doll's house, the painted box, the bed.

'In this house,' said Tolly, 'everything is twice!' He tried the lid of the painted box, but could not open it.

'The key is lost,' said Mrs Oldknow. 'I don't know what's in it. It used to be the children's toy-box.'

He put his hand on the rocking-horse's mane, which was real horse-hair. Its tail was real hair too, black and soft and long. He started it rocking. It made a nice creaky sound, like a rocking-chair. He opened the front of the doll's house. 'Why, it's this house!' he said. 'Look, here's the Knight's Hall, and here's the stairs, and here's my room! Here's the rocking-horse and here's the red box, and here's the tiny bird-cage! But it's got four beds in it. Are there sometimes other children here?'

Mrs Oldknow looked at him as if she would like to know everything about him before she answered.

'Yes,' she said, 'sometimes.'

'Who are they?'

'You'll see when they come, if they come.'

'When do they come?'

'When they like. Now let's unpack. Here are your pyjamas. Is there anything you want to have in bed with you – any books or photos that you put under your pillow?'

On the chest of drawers Tolly had seen two curly white china dogs, an old clock, and an ebony mouse, life-sized with shiny black eyes. It was so cleverly carved that you could see every hair, and it felt like fur to stroke. As he pulled the sheets up to his nose he said, 'Can I have the mouse in bed?'

Mrs Oldknow smiled. 'You want Toby's Japanese mouse? Here it is.'

'Who's Toby?'

'Well, really another Toseland. Toby for short. Now sleep well. I'll light the night-light for you. Oh, the clock's not going.'

She picked up the old clock, which had a sun and moon painted on its face, and started it ticking. It had a very slow tick-tock, comforting and sleepy. 'There,' she said. 'Now, good night. My room is underneath yours – you can knock on the floor if you want me.'

She went away, and Tolly lay happily looking at the surprising shadows made by the little night-light – the beams, the big shadow of the rocking-horse, the low one of the doll's house on the floor, the elongated wandering criss-crosses of the bird-cage on the ceiling. The mirror repeated it all in the opposite direction, distant and slightly tilted. How could such a little light do it all? Never in his life had he lain in such a room, yet it did not feel strange. He felt with all his heart that he was at home. He held the mouse in his hand under the pillow and soon fell asleep.

He slept long and well. In his dreams he was swimming towards the house in the dark when he heard the creak of oars coming to meet him. He tried to shout, but it was too difficult to do while swimming. In the effort he woke up. The funny thing was, that lying there with his eyes closed he could still hear the creak-croak. No, it couldn't be oars, it must be the rocking-horse. He sat up in bed, and it seemed to him that the horse had just that minute stopped rocking. The only sound he could hear now was the slow tick-tock of the old clock. The room was in dim half-light because the curtains were still drawn. Tolly jumped out of bed. First he put his precious mouse back between the two china dogs, then he went to the rocking-horse just to stroke its real silky mane, and to pretend to see if it was out of breath. Then he ran to the window and knelt on the window-seat behind the curtain to look out at the view he had not yet seen. When, just at that moment, Mrs Oldknow came into the room, all she could see of him was the soles of his pink feet. As she pulled back the curtain, he turned a happy excited face to her. 'Oh look! Oh look!' he said.

It was a brilliant, sunny morning, and all the view was sparkling blue water, right away to the low hills in the distance. From this high window he could see where the course of the river should be, because of the pollard willows sticking out along each side of the bank, and because there the water was whirlpooled and creased and very brown and swift, while all the miles of overflow were just like blue silk.

'It really is like being in the Ark,' said Tolly.

'Yes, all the children used to call it the Ark. Your grandfather did, and he learnt it from his father, who learnt it from his, and so on right away back. But you called it that by yourself.'

Tolly sat in his pyjamas on the rocking-horse, making it go creak-croak, creak-croak.

'Do you know,' he said, 'when I was lying in bed with my eyes shut I could hear the horse go creak-croak just like this? But when I opened my eyes it was quite still.'

'And did the mouse squeak under your pillow, and did the china dogs bark?'

'No,' said Tolly. 'Do they?'

Mrs Oldknow laughed. 'You seem ready for anything, that's something,' she said. 'Now get dressed and come down to breakfast.'

Tolly found his own way down the winding staircase, through the Music Room that was like a knight's hall, down the winding stairs again and across the entrance hall with its polished wooden children and queer sticks of flowers, and into the room where he had first met his great-grandmother the night before.

Breakfast was on the table, but she was standing by an open door throwing crumbs on to the doorstep for the birds. There were so many of them that they seemed to drop from the branches of the trees like ripe chestnuts when the tree is shaken, and as many were going up again with a piece of bread in their beaks as were coming down to get it. A few yards beyond the doorstep the garden was under water.

'The birds are very hungry. You see, they can't get worms, or seed, or ants' eggs until the floods go. Would you like to be introduced to them?'

'Yes please,' said Tolly.

'Come here, then,' said Mrs Oldknow; and although her back was rather bent and her face was wrinkled, when she looked at him so mischievously he could almost imagine she was a boy to play with. 'They love margarine better than anything,' she said. 'Hold out your hands.'

She spread his fingers and palms with margarine carefully all over, even between the fingers, then told him to go to the door and stand still, holding out both hands with the fingers open. She stood beside him and whistled. In a minute tits and robins and chaffinches and hedge-sparrows were fluttering round him till at last one ventured to perch on his thumb. After that the others were soon jostling to find room on his hands, fixing him with their bright eyes and opening their wings and cocking their tails to keep their balance. They pecked at the margarine on his palm and between his fingers. They tickled dreadfully, and Tolly wriggled

and squealed so that they all flew away, but in a
minute they were back.

'You must keep still and be quiet,' said Mrs Oldknow, laughing at him.

Tolly tried hard to obey her, but their beaks and
little wiry clutching hands felt so queer that he had to
shut his eyes and screw up his face to keep still. The tits
hung on underneath and tickled in unexpected places.

While he was standing there pulling faces he heard a
laugh so like a boy's that he could not believe his great-
grandmother had made it, and opened his eyes to see
who was there. There was no one else. Mrs Oldknow's
eyes were fixed on his. The blackbirds were scolding in
the branches because they were afraid to come on to his
hands and could see the margarine was nearly finished.
Then with a squabbling noise, like a crowd of rude
people off a football bus, a flock of starlings arrived,
snatching and pushing and behaving badly in every
way.

'That will do,' said Mrs Oldknow. 'Starlings don't
wait to be introduced to anybody. I'll give them some
bread, and you can wipe your hands on these crusts and
throw them to the blackbirds. Then run and wash your
hands.'

She shut the door and sat down to breakfast. Tolly
came quickly and sat down where a place was laid for
him opposite the fireplace.

While he was eating he was looking round again at
the room which was so different by daylight, though
just as unusual, with all its big windows looking out on

to water. Suddenly he saw something he had not noticed at all the night before, when the room had been full of firelight and shadows. Over the fireplace hung a large oil painting of a family, three children and two ladies. There were two handsome boys, wearing lace collars and dark green silk suits. They had long hair but looked anything but girlish. The elder of the two, who might be fourteen years old, was wearing a sword, and it looked so natural to him that Tolly was filled with hero-worship. He had his hand on the collar of a tame deer. The younger brother had a book under his arm and a flute in his hand. The little girl had a smile of irrepressible high spirits that seemed to defy the painter to do a serious portrait of her. She was holding a chaffinch, and beside her on the ground was an open wicker cage. One of the two ladies was young and beautiful. At her feet was a little curly white dog with a black face; on her arm a basket of roses. The other lady was old and dressed in black. They all had large dark eyes and all their eyes seemed fixed on Tolly. If he moved to one side all the eyes moved after him.

'Granny, they are all looking at me.'

'I'm not surprised. You have only just come. They must be tired of looking at me.'

'Who are they?'

'They are Oldknows. Your family. The boy with the deer is Toby, the other with the flute is Alexander, and the little girl is Linnet. She is six years old. That is their mother in the blue dress.'

'My mother was called Linnet,' said Tolly. 'And that's you behind them!'

'It's their grandmother, Mrs Oldknow.'

'Is this their house?'

'Yes, they lived here.'

'When did they live here?'

'Oh, a long time ago,' said Mrs Oldknow, fidgeting and being suddenly very busy about the breakfast table. But Tolly was only seven, and to him a long time ago meant more than seven years. Five lively pairs of eyes were challenging him to ignore them. Linnet was laughing straight into his. Even the dog looked as if it would play.

'Has Toby got a real sword?' he asked.

'Yes, of course.'

'Why?'

'Because he's going to be a soldier. His father gave it to him when he was thirteen.'

'Is Alexander going to be a musician?'

'He will go to the University. He wants to be a poet.'

'And Linnet?'

'My little Linnet –'

'Oh,' said Tolly, interrupting, 'that's the bird-cage in my room. It's the bird-cage in my room! It made such funny shadows on the ceiling when you put the night-light under it. Is the doll's house Linnet's?'

'No, the doll's house was mine when I was a little girl. I was brought up here by my uncle because I was an orphan.'

'Did you have brothers and sisters?'

'No; but I played that I had. I was lonely. That's why I put four beds in the doll's house.'

'Did you play that *they* were your brothers and sister?' said Tolly, pointing to the picture. Mrs Old-know looked hard at him.

'Yes, my dear. How did you know?'

'Because I think that is what I shall play. Do you want to read the newspapers now?'

'Good gracious no, child. What should I do that for? The world doesn't alter every day. As far as I can see, it's always the same. But I have plenty to do, so you must amuse yourself. Can you?'

'Oh, yes. I would like to go up to the rocking-horse and the mouse. Can I play with the cage if I can reach it?'

'You can play with anything you like if you are careful. Don't fall out of the window.' Tolly took two lumps of sugar from the bowl. 'For the horse,' he said. 'Can I?' He ran upstairs to his room as happy as a little boy could be.

First he pulled a chair under the wicker cage so that he could reach up to it. He opened the door, which made a little bird-like squeak as it turned on its hinges. He had nothing else to put in it, so he put the mouse inside and closed the door. He pretended to feed the horse with the sugar and put what was left over of it for the mouse. Then he groomed the horse all over with his hairbrush, particularly its mane and tail, and passed his hands down its legs as he had seen men do in stables, and talked to it all the time. He mounted it and started a long ride, creak–croak, pretending that Toby and Alexander and Linnet had invited him to visit them. 'Horses always know the way,' he said aloud. 'I expect it will take hours and hours.'

He was cheerfully rocking along, singing at the top of his voice a song his mother used to sing to him, before she died and the stepmother came.

> What is your one oh?
> Green grow the rushes oh
> What is your one oh?
> One is one and all alone
> And ever more shall be so.
> What are your two oh?
> Green grow the rushes oh
> What are your two oh?
> Two, two, the lily white boys
> Clothed all in green oh
> One is one and all alone
> And ever more shall be so.

Presently he heard tip-tap at one of the windows, and while he looked in that direction, tap-tap at the window behind him. It was a chaffinch knocking on the glass, for all the world as if it wanted to come in. Toseland dismounted and went over to see. Still it did not fly away, but held on to the cross-bars and tried first one pane and then another.

'Do you want to come in?' said Tolly, opening the window.

At once the bird flew in and perched on the cage. It hopped from one wicker strand to another, giving little excited calls until it found the door, which was shut. 'Cheep, cheep, cheep,' it scolded, and fluttered round the room, making a little sound of bird footsteps on the wooden floor when it hopped. Toseland opened the cage door, and the chaffinch flew straight across the room and into the cage. There it turned round and gave a little song, tried all the perches, hopping round to face both ways on each, swung in the swing, pecked at the sugar, and hopped out again on to Tolly's head. 'Don't,' said Tolly, shaking it. 'I don't like that. I can't see you.' The bird flew off on to the window-sill, looked round at him with a final chirp, and dived into a big tree near by, level with the window, where it perched and sang quietly to itself.

'Oh, come back, do come back, chaffinch! I wish I had some margarine. Perhaps sugar won't do. I wonder what Linnet used to put in the cage? Chaffinch! Chaffinch!'

The bird would not be coaxed, but when he had finished his song shot off across the water like an arrow and disappeared into a distant tree.

The floods had begun to go down. Already Tolly could see spikes of grass sticking up through the edge of the water. The shapes of lawns and flower-beds were showing through the ripples round the house. He longed for the water to go, so that he could explore the garden.

When he came downstairs for lunch, Boggis, in long wading boots, was bringing in logs for the fire, making a big stack of them in a corner of the inglenook.

'Good morning, Mr Boggis,' said Tolly. 'Have you come in the boat? I forgot to look last night to see what it was called.'

'It's called the *Linnet*, Master Toseland, but I didn't come in it today. I came in my waders. The water's going down lovely.'

'The *Linnet*?' said Toseland, turning to his great-grandmother.

'Yes,' she said. 'There's always a boat called *Linnet* on the river.'

'That's right,' said Boggis. 'There's always a *Linnet*. This one's new – leastways not more than twenty years old – but I used to go out in the old *Linnet* when I was a boy, and my grandfather used to talk about fishing at night with torches from the *Linnet* when he was young. See, ma'am, I've managed to borrow these from my niece whose boy is in hospital.' He held out two Wellingtons. 'I reckon Master Toseland will need these. Isn't he the fair spit of his grandfather! Might be the same come back.'

'Yes, he seems to belong here,' said Mrs Oldknow. 'He has it all hidden in him somewhere. I like to see him finding his way about.'

'Shall I take him out with me into the barn this afternoon while I cut wood, to keep him out of your way?'

'He's not in my way at all, but I expect he would like to go.'

'Oh yes, please!'

'Very well, Boggis, you can keep him till tea-time. Good-bye, Toby.'

'You said "Toby",' said Tolly, pulling on his borrowed Wellingtons.

'Why, so I did! I was forgetting.'

Boggis and Toseland paddled off side by side across the drive and turned into a walled yard that was now a walled lake, though you could see the cobbles through the shallow water, all different colours like pebbles at the sea-side. Along three sides there were buildings or sheds, very old and tumbledown. The longest had a row of arches, and over them bits of broken stone carving stuck out of the wall. Inside it was divided up into little rooms with scrolled iron doorways opening on to a passage. Some were filled with straw, some with faggots or peat. One was empty, and one had a wall ladder with hand and foot holes instead of rungs. Up this Boggis went, and through a trap-door above.

Tolly followed, and found himself in a room rather like his bedroom but much larger, smelling of hay and sawdust, and rich with a soft, musty kind of darkness. There was only one small round window covered with cobwebs, so that the light that came through was dove-grey. Here and there a ray of white light came slanting through a broken roof tile, against which you could see the golden motes of dust in the air. It looked mysterious and enticing. The floor made hollow noises and had holes in it where the boards had rotted. Up here Boggis had a bench and saw, and as he finished a log he

threw the pieces through the trap-door on to the floor
below.

In one of the little rooms downstairs Tolly had seen
a chair and table and a blue tea-pot and mug. 'Do you
live here?' he asked. Boggis looked at him with teasing
bright blue eyes. 'It all depends what you call living,'
he said. 'When I'm awake I'm mostly here, but when I
go home I mostly sleeps.'

'How long have you been here?'

'Fifty-five years. I came when I was twelve. But of
course I knew it before that because my father worked
here, same as me.'

'What are those little rooms downstairs with park
gates instead of doors?'

'Stables,' said Boggis briefly, out of breath with
sawing.

Tolly thought of the horses that had once lived in
such grand rooms.

'Were they very special horses?'

'Oh aye, they were fine horses when I was a lad.
Shining like the sun and dressed up like lords. I've
never had an overcoat like they had! When they were
led out, striking sparks out of the cobbles with their
hooves and shaking their bridles, they were a proper
eyeful. Your grandfather, Mr Toseland as was, he was
a rare one with a horse. He could make them do
anything by just breathing secrets into their ears.'

Boggis went on with his sawing, and Tolly roamed
round, his eyes getting used to the patchy light. He
found other trap-doors which he could not lift, a

whole row of them all along one side. One was broken and lay off its hinges beside the square hole. Underneath on the stable wall was the iron basket to hold hay, into which he climbed. He crouched there trying to imagine that the stall was occupied by the warm silky body of a horse, feet stamping in straw, hindquarters fidgeting, tail swishing, and a great rolling black eye that could see backwards and forwards at the same time, half covered by mane and forelock. He tried so passionately to imagine it, to see, hear and smell it, that the wonder is that no horse was there.

'Hullo there! Master Toseland, where are you?'

'I'm here,' he answered, standing up so that his head stuck out of the hole.

'Trust you to get in the haunted stall! Were you looking for Mr Toby's horse by any chance? That stall's always kept empty in case he feels like spending a night there. Folk say you can hear him at night, whinnying for the young master.'

'Which young master?'

'Don't ask me! I bain't no good at history. One of the young masters, same as you.'

'Have you ever heard him whinnying?'

Boggis cocked a half-humorous, half-serious eye at him. 'I tells you, I sleeps at home. And that's where I dreams.'

Toseland climbed over the hayrack and let himself down into the manger.

'You haven't put any hay for him,' he said.

'Ghosts don't eat hay.'

'But they like to pretend.'

The manger was empty. It was as big as a bed and he could lie full length in it. In that position, running his fingers along the cracks, he found a loose piece of wood wedged under the ledge of the manger at the back. Just for love of poking round, Toseland, with great difficulty, prized it out. On one side of it there was dirty paint. He rubbed it with his sleeve and saw that there were red and white patterns on it. He licked his handkerchief and rubbed harder. Some letters appeared, very queer spiky, spidery letters, not like print at all.

'Mr Boggis, look what I've found.'

Boggis came and peered through the trap-door.

'Now then, don't you take away nothing you finds here. We don't want no souvenir hunting here.'

Toseland put it down in the bottom of the manger. There ought to be hay, he thought. Of course they ought to put hay. Then he remembered that he still had a piece of sugar that he had taken for the rocking-horse. He put it carefully exactly in the middle of the painted board. Then he climbed down from the manger and ran up the ladder again to the loft. It was getting so dark that by now Boggis had lit his storm-lantern to finish his sawing. The loft looked even more exciting by lamplight, but in another quarter of an hour Boggis said it was tea-time – time to go in.

Toseland walked in front with the lantern, and they stepped from the stables into shallow water and waded slowly towards the house. As they went under the big yew trees the lantern lit up the underneath of the branches making them look like rafters in wild magic houses. The windows of Green Noah were all lit up again. Tolly felt as if he had lived here always instead of just one day.

Mrs Oldknow was sitting in front of a tea-tray by the fire, just as before, when Tolly came in all dirty with bits of straw in his hair.

'I can see where you've been,' she said. 'Go and wash yourself and get the straw out of your hair; then come and tell me all about it. I can see you are bursting with questions again.'

When he came back she said: 'Show me your hands. And now turn round and let me see if you have got peat dust on the seat of your trousers. There! Now begin. Here's some hot buttered toast and honey.'

'Granny, what was the name of Toby's special horse?'

Mrs Oldknow put down her cup and saucer. 'Boggis has been telling you stories.'

'Yes, and I found something.'

'Toby's horse was called Feste. What did you find?'

'I found a funny board with patterns and writing on it. It looked like a name but I couldn't read it. It was funny writing.'

'It was a name. Feste. Good boy, you are doing well! I thought that board was lost – that someone had chopped it up by mistake, or on purpose. I haven't seen it since I was married. When the stables were built each horse had its name above the manger. Alexander had a white pony called Bucephalus. Poor little Linnet wasn't allowed a horse of her own. She rode in a pannier behind her mother or Boggis – I mean the Boggis there was then.'

'Granny, I do want to hear Feste neigh. Is my bedroom too far away to hear him – if he did, I mean?'

She smiled gently at him. 'No, I don't think it's too far away.'

'Did you hear him when you were little?'

'Oh, yes, I heard him. Generally at sundown. There were other horses then, of course, but I could always tell Feste's voice. It is quite individual.'

There was a long silence while Toseland imagined having a horse of his own, even a ghost horse.

'I did a silly thing,' he said at last. 'I put a lump of sugar for him.'

'That wasn't silly at all, darling,' she said.

'Granny, what did Linnet put in the bird-cage? The chaffinch didn't like sugar. He came, you know, but he wouldn't stay.'

'Linnet always left the door open. She didn't like to shut them in. She put crumbs of pastry and biscuit, and seeds that she gathered in the garden in the summer. The chaffinches came and went as they liked, but they always built their nest in the cage in spring. She put a forked branch of hawthorn for them. You can do that too. I am surprised they have remembered for so long; no one has used that room for years. I think they must tell stories to their nestlings.'

'Stories about Linnet, as you do to me?'

'Why not?'

'Tell me more about them, please. Why isn't their father there in the picture?'

'He was a ship's captain. There was an older boy too, Aubrey, who was a midshipman on his father's ship. Captain Oldknow sailed all over the world. He used to bring home presents for the family. From one journey he brought the mouse for Toby – your mouse – and that great silk Chinese lantern that hangs in the Music Room for his wife. It opens and shuts like an umbrella, but I never touch it now because the silk is so old and tender. Alexander and Linnet were not born then.'

'What else did he bring home?'

'From Holland he brought all that lovely lace that they are wearing, and the bird-cage; from Spain, Toby's sword; and from Germany, the book that Alexander's holding.'

'How could he read it if it was a German book?'

'It was in Latin and he could read it, and he loved it. From France he brought that little dog for Linnet and a lot of rose trees for his wife. Those are the flowers in her basket. Roses were almost a new discovery, very fashionable and exciting. Everybody wanted to have some. They are growing here in the garden still.'

'The same ones?'

'The same in a way, descended from them as you are from the captain.'

'I feel as though I had lived here always,' said Toseland. 'Why is it called Green Noah?'

Mrs Oldknow's faced suddenly creased into rings of unhappy wrinkles.

'For someone who's lived here always, you ask a lot of questions,' she said.

'I know, Granny. But tell me, please.'

'It's not the real name,' she said. 'It used to be called Green Knowe, but it – got changed. A long time ago.' That was all she would say. But Tolly had more questions.

'You know,' he said, 'all those children's faces carved in wood in the entrance hall? They all seemed to be laughing when I came. Who put them there?'

This time Mrs Oldknow looked pleased. 'The grandmother in the picture found them in a builder's store. They came from the chapel of a monastery that had been pulled down. She bought them for the beams in the children's bedroom. She said they were guardian angels. Now, as you see, they are welcoming angels – though one was guardian to a chaffinch last year.'

'What colour was Feste?'

'He was chestnut with a white nose and four white feet like a kitten, and he jumped like a cat. Toby and he loved each other more than anything on earth.'

'But the deer was Toby's too,' said Tolly, gazing at the picture. 'Isn't it beautiful! A deer seems more magic than a horse.'

'Very beautiful fairy-tale magic, but a horse that thinks the same thoughts that you do is like strong magic wine, a love philtre for boys.'

*

Tolly lay awake in bed. There was so much to think about – the birds, the children, the floods, the stables where lovely Feste called for his master. It was a clear night with a full moon shining on miles of water and seeming twice as bright as usual. The bedroom was all silver and black with it as it poured through the window and flooded the floor with quicksilver. The flame of the night-light looked like a little golden pen-nib, giving less light than there was already around it. The moon shone in the rocking-horse's eye, and in the mouse's eye too when Tolly fetched it out from under his pillow to see. The clock went tick-tock, and in the stillness he thought he heard little bare feet running across the floor, then laughter and whispering, and a sound like the pages of a big book being turned over.

'It might be Alexander and Linnet looking at pictures by moonlight,' he thought, dreamily. 'But where are they?'

He sat up and stared all round the room. There was only his own bed and all his things just as he had left them, clearly seen in the moonlight, though there were black patches of shadow under the window where he could not see. Then there was all the room repeated in the looking-glass, more mysterious, the moonlit parts brighter, the dark more impenetrable. The whispering went on. If they were in the dark corners, he thought, they couldn't see the pictures.

'Linnet!' he called suddenly. 'Where are you? Come out into the moonlight.'

There was a laugh just where he wasn't looking, and when he turned that way, a patter of feet, and the whispering was where he had been looking a moment before.

'Are you just teasing me?' he asked, and was answered by such an infectious little laugh that he couldn't help laughing too. After that there was silence, but it was a companionable, happy one in which presently he smiled and settled himself to sleep. He dreamed that he was holding out his hands dripping with golden syrup, and that it was Feste who came with his soft white nose and pinky-grey lips and sucked it all off, while Linnet flew in the air like a bird and laughed from the branches of the trees.

When he woke Mrs Oldknow was standing by his bed smiling at him.

'It's time to get up. Look, the floods have all gone in the night. Come and see.' She opened the window to lean out. 'Tolly! Quick! Quick!'

Under the high window all the lawns were emerald green. Beyond them the river flowed obediently in its own course, and beyond that again were miles of green meadow. Right in front of the window where the last pool was draining away from a hollow in the grass, a large silvery thing was twisting and jumping violently in the sun.

'It's a great big fish.'

'It's one of Toby's carp from the moat. Silly thing – it got left behind when the water went away. Run, Tolly, put on your coat and your Wellingtons and throw it back into the moat.'

Tolly ran as fast as he could, slithering down the steep winding stairs in his socks and pulling on his Wellingtons by the front door. He reached the fish before anyone else, but it was nearly as big as himself, and flapped so wildly when he picked it up that he was afraid and let it fall again. Then it gasped horribly and lay still, and now he was afraid to touch it in case it was dying. Just then Boggis arrived with a wheelbarrow.

'Quick, quick, Mr Boggis! It's Toby's fish. It's dying! It's Toby's! Mr Boggis, quick!'

Boggis came without any hurry and bent his bright red face down to look.

'Ay, it's one of Master Toby's sure enough. What a size it have grown to! Must be hundreds of years old.'

He put the fish in his barrow and led Tolly to the moat, which was a ring of deep water all round the garden. There he tipped the barrow up and the fish plopped in and disappeared. They stood and looked at the place where it had fallen.

'Was it still alive?' asked Tolly. As he spoke, a fish face was poked above the surface, then there was a swirl of water, a flip of a tail, and it was gone.

'Sure enough it was!' said Boggis.

'It was a very ugly fish,' said Toseland.

'T'aint no beauty. No more will you be when you're a hundred years old! Master Toby used to feed it with bread.'

'It came when he called it,' added Mrs Oldknow, joining them. 'Its name is Neptune. Toby used to tell

Linnet that it understood Latin. He always talked to it in Latin. She was very much impressed.'

'What did he say to it?'

'He said "*Veni Neptune. Panem dabo tibi et vermes*".'

'I don't know any Latin.'

'Neither did Linnet. It means "Come Neptune. I will give you bread and worms". In the garden you will find a platform over a pool where he fed them.'

They fed the birds together. Tolly wanted his hands to be buttered again, but was told that that was only for the introduction ceremony, not for every day.

'Do the birds understand Latin?'

'No, not Latin. Music. Alexander used to play the flute to them. They used to sing when he played, but all different tunes. Only the thrushes learnt his tune and the starlings who never sang it properly – they only made fun of it.'

'What tune did the thrushes sing?'

'"Greensleeves", for one.'

'Oh Granny, I know "Greensleeves". I do really. At school we had it on the wireless. I wish I had a flute.'

'Perhaps you'll get one for Christmas. That's quite soon, you know. Now finish your breakfast and then you can explore the garden.'

The garden had looked very desolate when the water was over it, but now even the trees looked different and every path seemed to lead just where it was most exciting to go. First he went round the east corner of the house that he had not yet seen. Broken stones stuck out all up the wall, as if there had once been a building there that had been pulled down. In fact there was still a high garden wall with arched slits in it that must once have been windows. Ferns and shrubs and ivy were growing out of the cracks between the stones and there was a lovely smell in the air. Quite suddenly he became aware of something so big that at first he had not seen it.

Against the side of the house, immensely tall and half covered with festoons of Old Man's Beard, was a stone figure. The first thing that attracted his attention to it was, close to the ground, some stone fishes swimming in what looked like stone water, as though the flood had left something behind. Then he saw that behind the fishes were two huge bare stone feet that seemed to be paddling with stone ripples round the ankles; above them, legs and folds of clothing. High above that, so that he had to step back to look up at it, among the twining strings of the creeper he saw the head of a giant stone man, carrying a child on his shoulders.

Tolly was astonished. He looked and looked at it and could not go away. He played round its feet for a long time, collecting coloured pebbles out of the gravel, and stones that were like different things, such as a peg-top, an egg, a calf's face, a hammer-head; and a real marble. Every now and then he would look up to see the statue again. Its surface was worn soft by rain and frost and wind, not shiny and hard like monuments in churches. It looked friendly and nearly alive. Tolly loved it.

At last curiosity led him away to see where the other paths would lead him. There were many big trees and wild places where there were only little paths like rabbit runs. As he went along the birds went with him. They whistled and chirped on every side and always flew out of the bushes just before he arrived there, to perch on others just ahead. He followed a track round the edge of the moat, shuffling his feet in the dead leaves and pine-needles and stooping under low branches. Here, in a little clearing between two huge trees he found his next great surprise.

Standing on the grass with its ears pricked up as if it had just heard him was a deer that was a bush. It was like Toby's deer in the picture, but cut out of live evergreen with brown bush-stalk legs growing out of the ground. Toseland stroked it; its neck felt soft. It seemed so much alive that it was queer that of course it couldn't have eyes. How wild it looks without eyes, he thought. How magic! It took his breath away. And then he saw, sitting under a big beech tree, a green yew squirrel with a high tail. That seemed to be listening too. Other living things beside the birds were rustling in the bushes, and he heard other calls, more like children than birds. Tolly ran, hoping to catch them. He found nothing but a live rabbit that bolted in long hops and shot down a hole. He ran on down the little path, past a yew peacock – that was comparatively ordinary. Further on there was a green hare sitting very erect by the water's edge; then the path suddenly turned and left the water, going by a bank of trees and dense undergrowth and brambles where it would be almost impossible to walk. It came out between a yew cock and hen, on to a large lawn.

Tolly wanted to get back to the water again, and by-and-by he found a flight of steps which led down towards it. Here the moat formed a deep pool over-shadowed by trees, though now it was winter and the branches were bare except for the birds that had fol-lowed him and perched there. The water was brown with a blue gloss reflected on it from the sky, like a starling's back. The steps ended in a wooden platform. As Tolly stood and looked into the water he thought he saw, deep down, a great, shadowy fish swimming slowly. This, then, was Toby's platform.

Tolly tried to remember the Latin, but he knew it was hopeless. He would only make silly noises and the fish would know it was wrong. Just then something fell in the water. He couldn't see what it was because it sank and wobbled as it went down, but the old carp rose slowly to meet it and opened his mouth to suck it in. Then he sank again out of sight. What can that have been, thought Toseland. Perhaps a greedy blackbird took more breakfast than it could eat and threw its last crust away. And yet I don't believe that. It couldn't have tut-tutted and called so much if its mouth was full.

He began to retrace his steps, and now in the wood path he was sure there were others beside himself. Of course, he thought suddenly. It's hide-and-seek! 'Cooee!' he called. 'The Green Deer is den!' He ran as fast as he could till he stopped, out of breath, with his arms round the Green Deer's neck. Then he heard unmistakable breathless laughter quite close to him and felt something on his head. He put his hand up and found a twig. It was not something that could have fallen off any of the trees round him. It was cut out of a reddish bush and made a perfect T.

When he got back to the house he turned for another look at the stone man. Mrs Oldknow was there with some garden scissors cutting branches off the shrubs, which he now noticed with a little disappointment were covered with the peculiar flowers he had first seen in the entrance hall.

'When I first came,' he said, 'I thought those were magic flowers in the hall.'

'So you were afraid I was a witch?'

'Yes, before I saw you.'

'Well, this flower *is* called Witchhazel. And this is Winter Sweet, and that is Daphne. She was turned into a bush, you know.' Mrs Oldknow, who saw everything, was looking at the twig T in his hand. 'You found the Green Deer? And somebody's been teasing you, I see. When I was little I used to find a twig L in my lap. You see, my Christian name is Linnet.'

'Did they play hide-and-seek with you?'

'Yes.'

Toseland was looking at the stone man. 'Who is he?'

'He is our own St Christopher, and these ruins are where his chapel stood until some stupid wretch pulled it down. There is always a St Christopher by an old ford, and the ford across this river was at the end of the garden. You know the story? He carried the infant Jesus across in a storm, thinking it would be easy, but halfway across he began to feel the child as heavy as the sorrow of the whole world. Linnet loved St Christopher quite specially. She always liked to play here. I planted what you thought were magic flowers for winter incense. This is my favourite part of the garden too. Now, tell me where you've been this morning?'

'I've seen the Green Deer and all the other green things.'

'*All?* Which have you seen?'

'The deer and the squirrel and the peacock and the hare and the cock and the hen.'

Mrs Oldknow seemed relieved. 'And what else?'

'And I found Toby's steps by the water. And I saw the fish again. And *they* played hide-and-seek.'

Tolly was glad that Mrs Oldknow seemed not at all surprised by the hide-and-seek. He was not quite sure whether she thought that he and she were playing a game together pretending that there were other children, or whether she thought, as he did, that the children were really there.

In the afternoon he went back to the stables to look in Feste's manger. The sugar had gone! Toseland put another lump in its place and slipped away again so that it might be eaten quickly in private. Boggis had gone out on a message for Mrs Oldknow, and she herself was writing letters, so Tolly was alone again, but he had almost forgotten that it was sometimes dull. He went back to the Green Deer full of expectation, but all the birds seemed asleep and there was not a sound anywhere. The Green Deer did not seem magic now. It was not listening, its eyelessness was just stupid, not an added sense. The squirrel also was only a bush cut to shape. Tolly had come with an excited imagination. He collected beech–nuts and put them before the squirrel, and handfuls of dry hay for the deer, but it turned out only a dull make-believe. Nothing moved, nothing happened. All his interest faded away. He could think of nothing to do alone and as the afternoon wore on he felt lonely and neglected. He went back to the stables, but they were only empty buildings. There was no echo, there was nothing, there was nobody. When it began to get dark he went indoors. Mrs Oldknow was getting the tea ready.

'Can I come in now?' he asked. She looked at him quickly and saw at once what was the matter.

'Yes, come in, darling. You've been alone quite long enough, and so have I. It's been one of those afternoons when nothing will come alive. I know them. Sit down there opposite your friends, and after tea we'll see what we can do together. Did you see your chaffinch today?'

'Oh!' said Toseland, very much ashamed, 'I forgot to put anything for him. Suppose he's been tapping and tapping at the window and nobody came. Will he come again, do you think?'

'Try shortbread crumbs and see if that pleases him tomorrow morning. He might have spent all afternoon with you if you hadn't forgotten him.'

Tolly felt in a better temper already. 'Who made all the green animals?' he asked.

'Boggis's grandfather. They were there when I was a

child, and when I asked him about them he said the children wanted them for the Ark. There weren't any children living here then; my cousins were all much older than me. But at the time I thought I knew what he meant. He was very like our Boggis, but his face was redder and his eyes were bluer, and he dearly loved the bottle.'

'Did they have a tame squirrel?'

'They tamed everything. They seemed to understand animals. The hare used to come into the house, lolloping up and down stairs after Toby, or standing up to look out of the windows to see where he had gone. It was called Watt.'

When they had finished their tea Mrs Oldknow said: 'Make up a great blaze, Tolly, and then let's put the lights out and sit here, and I will tell you a story.' Tolly made a crackling fire, using the big leather bellows. There was a tear in one side, so that when they sucked in, the fire grew crimson and tried to follow the draught up the nozzle; when they blew out, the flames turned primrose and blue and sparks flew up as if from a Catherine-wheel. Then he blew out all the candles and came and settled himself at her feet.

'What shall it be about?'

'Tell me a story about Feste, please.'

Toby's Story

Once upon a time, when the floods were out and most of the country was under water, Linnet fell ill. Her mother would have liked to call in the doctor, but he lived many miles away on the other side of the river. There was no telephone in those days, so somebody would have to be sent to tell him.

'What shall I do?' said Linnet's mother. 'Boggis has broken his leg and he can't ride. The stable-boy is a young fool. I would never trust a horse to him alone on flooded roads.'

'Let me go,' said Toby. 'Feste and I would be quite trustworthy.'

'No, no,' said his mother. 'I should be more anxious about you than I am about Linnet. We will see if Grandmother's remedies will cure her.'

Their grandmother was very skilled in nursing, and kept a cupboard full of herbal medicines which she made herself, for every childish illness. Though she had done everything she could throughout the day, towards evening Linnet's fever was higher than ever. She lay with scarlet cheeks tossing in bed and talking as if she did not know what she said, so that the tears ran down her mother's face as she heard it.

'Mother, let me go for the doctor,' said Toby again.

'Dear boy,' said his mother, 'if I had let you go at first all might have been well. But now it is growing dark and who knows how the water is rising?'

'Feste can see in the dark, Mother. The dark does not frighten me, but it frightens me to see Linnet so ill.'

'He is right,' said the grandmother. 'Let him go. Feste will look after him.'

'You may ride to our neighbour the farmer, and tell him, I beg him to ride for the doctor at Potto Fen,' said his mother.

'The farmer may be away, or unable, or unwilling, and that would be so much time wasted, Mother. I will go quickly, and the doctor can be here this evening.'

Just then Linnet began to moan. She sat up in bed as if greatly distressed, and fell back on her pillow with her eyes open but seeing nothing. Her mother was distracted.

'Yes, Toby, go. Go quickly. But take care. Go the

shortest way over the wooden bridge and up the hill. Tell him it is very urgent.'

Toby pulled on his long, loose-topped boots and took his thick cloak and ran down to the stables. He saddled Feste, and as he put on the bridle he talked to him, saying, 'Feste, we must get the doctor for Linnet.'

The horse, who had lowered his head to receive the bridle, nuzzled Toby's cheek and understood very well that he was troubled. He gave a little neigh, and as soon as Toby's leg was over the saddle he whisked round and started off. It was not dark yet, the sky was dim green like water, and shallow water was over the roads. As they cantered off the mud flew up like a dirty fountain round them. The lane took them for four miles and ended at the wooden bridge. The river looked very nasty in the half light. The current heaved and pushed and the middle of the river seemed higher than the sides, as if it had been squashed up. The bridge was still well above the water.

Toby pulled his horse to a walking pace lest the wood should be slippery, and expected that Feste would cross it as he had done hundreds of times before. But no; Feste, the obedient, would not cross it. He sidled and waltzed but he would not go on. Toby talked to him, coaxed him, scolded him, pulling his head round to face the bridge again and again, but all in vain. At last, for the first time in his life he lifted his switch and lashed him. Feste reared up and struck at the air with outstretched fore-feet so that it was all Toby could do to hang on in the saddle. When in this way Feste had exhibited his height and his strength and his angry pride, he came down from his prancing and without warning leapt the high hedge at the side of the lane. He slithered down the bank with his fore-feet stuck out before him, and after sidling some distance along the river bank he trumpeted a challenging neigh and, plunging into the cold ugly river, began to swim.

Toby could feel the powerful water buffeting and shoving his leg on the upstream side, dragging and snatching at it on the other. It was as though the river were determined to separate him from Feste. Now and then a branch would hit him as a broken tree went past. Once they were tangled up in some floating straw from a rick. It nearly carried Toby out of the saddle, but he just managed to push it away. As they swam, they were swept gradually downstream towards the bridge. Toby, crouched over Feste's labouring shoulders, could feel that he was striking out for his life. His ears were straining forward and his eyes too, so that Toby could see the whites, and he snorted and grunted with his muzzle just above the water.

They reached the farther bank only a few yards upstream from the bridge, and scrambled up on the other side, Feste digging in with his toes while he gathered his hocks for the last great effort. At the top of the bank he stood with heaving sides and trembling shoulders shaking his heavy wet mane and hanging his head.

'Feste, you mad, crazy horse! Whatever possessed you to do that?' gasped Toby, twisting in the saddle to pull off his loose boots one by one to empty the water out of them. He was soaked to the neck and bitterly cold. His teeth chattered and his hands were blue. 'Stand, Feste, stand, you madman! The devil's in you!'

Feste was backing away from the bridge and flinging his head up and down so that Toby had to give up trying to wring water out of his cloak.

Suddenly there came a hair-raising scream, the scream of rending wood, sounding almost like an animal in panic. The wooden bridge twisted and cockled under his eyes and, with cracks like cannon fire, collapsed and was swept in a tangled mass downstream. Feste screamed too, and they were off together at full gallop up the hill in the fading light.

Feste chose his own way, jumping fences, jumping hedges, sloshing and slithering in the mud, but Toby did not interfere with him again. He gave him his head and was only concerned to stay with him. At last he recognized the outskirts of the village where the doctor lived. They rattled down the cobbled streets and it seemed to Toby that Feste stopped at the house of his own accord.

When the old doctor came to the door and saw the two of them standing dripping there, with their long hair plastered over their white faces, their coats covered with mud, he did not at first recognize them.

'What in Heaven's name!' he exclaimed. 'You're no bearer of good news. Martha! Bring the lantern. Why, here's young Master Oldknow in a fine state.'

The housekeeper came running with the lantern.

'Lord sakes, Master Toby, what brings you here like this?'

'Oh, sir, Linnet is ill of a high fever and cannot breathe. My mother begs you to make haste.'

'I can believe she's ill if your mother sends you through the floods for me. Martha, call the groom. Tell him to saddle the mare at once.'

'You must go round by Penny Soaky, sir,' said Toby, getting his breath again. 'The wooden bridge is down. Feste would not cross it, he chose to swim instead, and it crumpled up and went downstream just as we got to the other side. Feste knew. And the bridge screamed like demons.'

'Eh! Eh! What's this? You swam the river?' The jolly old doctor looked quite grey at the thought. Then he began to twinkle. 'So Feste chose to swim, did he? Do you let your horses choose, young man? I thought you knew more horsemanship than that.'

'He's never disobeyed me before, sir. And the worst of it is, I slashed him for it.'

'You go in, young man, and Martha will give you a hot grog and put you to bed while she dries your clothes. And as soon as I've gone, the groom shall see to Feste.'

'I'd like to see to Feste myself, sir. Nobody grooms him but me, and tonight especially I must, please.'

'Very well. But you can't stay in those clothes. You'll have to wear some of mine – or Martha's, whichever you please.'

Toby laughed, for both of them were as fat as barrels. 'I'll wear yours, thank you, sir.'

'As you please, young man. And then you go to bed and I'll tell your mother you'll be back tomorrow. I'll want to look at you myself before you go.'

The groom came round with the doctor's sedate mare, and Martha with hot grog for Toby.

'See that this young gentleman has everything he wants for his horse. And Martha, rig him up in anything of mine that he can stand up in. Good-bye, Toby, I'll see to your sister for you.'

It was no good trying to put the doctor's thick, voluminous clothes on Toby's slim body. He was so encumbered by the folds that it would have been impossible for him to do anything but trip over them. In the end he took a sleeveless jerkin that came down below his knees. He belted in its fantastic width like a kilt, and calling out: 'Way for Jamie Stuart, King of Scotland!' he ran barefooted out to Feste, who was tied up in a strange stable, whinnying for him again and again.

First he washed the four white feet in a bucket of warm water. Then he rubbed him hard with clean straw to get the mud off his coat and warm him by friction. Then he rubbed him with a cloth till he was dry all over, behind the ears, between his forelegs and round his fetlocks. He covered him with warm blankets and belted a coat round him.

All the while he talked to him, saying, 'Oh, my wonderful Feste, my golden eagle, my powerful otter, my wise horse.' As he combed the long mane, he sang as he had learned to do in church: *'Behold, thou art fair, my love, behold thou art fair. Thine eyes are as dove's eyes within thy locks. Thy neck is like the tower of David builded for an armoury, whereon there hang a thousand bucklers, all shields of mighty men.'*

When Feste was dry, shining and beautiful again, he was given a hot bran mash. Toby could not bear to leave him, but sat against the wall watching with great satisfaction how Feste sucked up from the bucket and how the level in the bucket went down and down. When it was all gone, Feste gave the bucket a push with his nose and a knock with his hoof, and lifted up his dripping muzzle towards Toby.

'Feste, you're a messy eater,' he said, carefully wiping the horse's chin with one of the doctor's handkerchiefs. Feste gave a great sigh and began to bend his knees and his hocks to lie down. Down he went in his straw bed and curled himself up like a dog with his nose tucked into his legs.

Toby sat on, meaning just to watch him go to sleep. But he fell asleep himself. When the groom came in to see if everything was in order for the night, he found the young gentleman asleep with his head against the horse's neck. He approached to wake him up, to take him into the house, but Feste opened a rolling eye and put his ears back with a dangerous look, making it quite plain that no one was to disturb either of them.

The groom hesitated, then he went out and brought back two more blankets that he spread over Toby. Feste opened an eye, but did not move. When the groom had gone he sighed and shut it again. So there they slept together. The next thing that Toby knew was that Feste was blowing down his neck as if to say: 'That supper was splendid, but how about breakfast?'

Tolly woke early next morning, still excited with the knowledge that the world into which he was born had once produced a Feste. He lay for a moment with his eyes shut, listening for any sound there might be in the room. The slow tick-tock came out of the silence, and then a soft whirring followed by the little tap of a bird perching, and lastly, sounding very loud because it was near his ear, a scratching of bird-claws on his sheet and the tiny bump of a bird's hop on his chest. When he opened his eyes he looked straight into the round black eye of the chaffinch.

It gave a loud chirp, as if it were making an important statement, something like 'I'm as good as you are', but with no boastfulness, only friendly confidence. Then it flew out of the window. In a moment it was back. 'I'm as good as you are' it said, and went into the cage for the last of the pastry crumbs.

It hopped round the room examining everything with its head tipped sideways as if its eye were a spotlight. It tugged at Toseland's shoe-laces, picked up his Twig T that he had put carefully by his bed, tried to fly away with it, but found it too heavy and threw it away. In front of the big mirror it bowed to its own reflection, announced as usual 'I'm as good as you are' and seemed to wait for a reply. Getting none, it flew out of the window again.

'How quickly it makes up its mind about everything,' thought Toseland, getting out of bed and climbing on to the rocking-horse. He worked hard, making it rear high and higher until it stood right up on its hind-legs and he had to clutch it round the neck and lean forward to bring it down again. 'My golden eagle, my wise horse, my powerful otter,' he chanted as he rocked. Before he went down to breakfast he brushed its mane and tail and put two rugs over it, belting them round with the strap of his trunk.

He went to the bed to get his mouse from under the pillow. As his hand closed over it, it felt warm to his touch, and with surprise he saw pastry crumbs in the bed. Suddenly he remembered Mrs Oldknow's question: 'And did the mouse squeak and the dogs bark?'

'Mouse, mouse,' he said, looking into its shiny black eye, 'where have you been? This house is full of shiny black eyes, all looking at me.'

As he went down the winding wooden stairs he heard someone whistling in his bedroom behind him. A bird? He turned his head to listen, but what he heard was laughter in the Music Room below him. He pelted down the stairs, making a great noise with his shoes, but by then children's voices came from his great-grandmother's room beyond.

Mrs Oldknow was there, turning her head and bending down as if she were listening to a child that was clutching her skirts. She looked up with a queer smile as Tolly came in, rather as if she had been caught. 'What a hurry you are in for breakfast this morning!

Pelting down your stairs as if you were chasing butter-flies.' Toseland had a feeling that she was hiding some-thing from him. The voices and laughter had vanished.

All that day it seemed that the children were deter-mined to tease Tolly. In the house, in the garden, wherever he was not, they were. They sounded so happy, so full of games and high spirits that Tolly, in spite of all disappointments, still ran towards it when he heard 'cooee' in the garden, or stopped and crept stealthily round a corner when he heard whispering. But he found no one. While he was loitering round St Christopher's feet he was playfully pelted with beech-nuts through the window-opening in the garden wall. When he visited the Green Deer he found twigs on the ground arranged like arrows pointing a trail. He fol-lowed these past the green squirrel, the green hare, the peacock, and the cock and hen, till he arrived at the fish platform. There all he found was more twigs arranged to form the letters T, A, L. He broke off two more and put another T underneath. There was a little dog barking somewhere, rather muffled as if someone were trying to keep it quiet.

He visited Feste's stall, walking in on tiptoe as some people do in church. The sugar was gone again! Joyfully he put another piece.

He felt very good-tempered all morning, but by the middle of the afternoon he had forgotten that yesterday he had been dull because there was no hide-and-seek. Now he was cross because there was too much of it.

'I hate hide-and-seek when you never find anybody,'

he said to himself. 'It's a perfectly horrid game.' He walked to the house kicking sticks and stones as he went. He even felt inclined to kick St Christopher, but stopped in time and was ashamed of having such a thought.

As he went along the entrance hall, past one of the big mirrors, something in it caught his eye. It looked like a pink hand. The glass reflected a dark doorway on the other side of the stairs. Behind the door-post, flattened against the wall on tiptoe to make themselves as thin as they could, their faces puckered with holding in their laughter, he saw Linnet and Alexander. It was Linnet's hand on the door-post. Their black eyes were fixed on him. There was no mistake, he knew them.

'I spy!' he shouted, whisking round to chase them, but they did not run away, they simply vanished.

He felt the wall where they had been; he looked all round. He ran out to the Green Deer, but the clearing was empty and quiet. Certainly the Green Deer looked magic enough, ready to spring away. The light was queer too, the sky was dark green, the wind dead. Tolly was half frightened. Something was going to happen.

As he looked up at St Christopher's face a snowflake drifted past it, then another, and suddenly it was snowing thickly. Like millions of tiny white birds circling home to roost, the flakes danced in the air. They filled the sky as far up as he could imagine. At the same time all the sounds in the world ceased. The snow was piling up on the branches, on the walls, on the ground, on St

Christopher's face and shoulders, without any sound at all, softer than the thin spray of fountains, or falling leaves, or butterflies against a window, or wood ash dropping, or hair when the barber cuts it. Yet when a flake landed on his cheek it was heavy. He felt the splosh but could not hear it.

He went in plastered with snow, and here tea was ready, with Mrs Oldknow sitting by the fire waiting for him. In the fire the snow drifting down the chimney was making the only noise it ever can – a sound like the striking of fairy matches; though sometimes when the wind blows you can hear the snow like a gloved hand laid against the window.

Tolly made the toast and his great-grandmother spread it with honey. They talked about Christmas. Mrs Oldknow said Boggis was going to buy the tree the next day, unless they were snowed up. Tolly hoped they would be. He liked the idea of being snowed up in a castle. By the light of the candles he could see the flakes drifting past the windows.

'What will the birds do?' he asked.

'They do not mind the snow so long as we feed them. Is your window open enough for the chaffinch to get in? Take some shortbread and make him welcome.' Tolly did as she said. When he came down again the curtains were all drawn, and he settled down by the fire in hopes of another story.

'Granny, both my pieces of sugar have gone out of Feste's stall.'

'Perhaps Boggis takes them and puts them in his tea,' she said, laughing.

Tolly's face fell. He had never thought of anything so low-down, so common. He was shattered.

At that moment, while Mrs Oldknow was still laughing at him, outside the door that led into the garden someone began a Christmas carol. Children's voices, delicate and expert, were singing 'The Holly and the Ivy'. Tolly had never heard such beautiful singing. He listened entranced.

> O the rising of the sun
> The running of the deer
> The playing of the merrie organ
> Sweet singing in the choir.

'What will they sing next?' he asked in a whisper, and waited in silence. 'I Saw Three Ships Come Sailing By' was the next, and then a carol Tolly did not know, which began, 'Tomorrow shall be my dancing day' and which ended:

> Sing O my love, my love, my love, my love,
> This have I done for my true love.

When that was finished there was a pause and a little girl's laugh – ah, he knew that laugh now! Mrs Oldknow's eyes were fixed on him and she saw him start.

'Shall we let them in?' she asked. Tolly nodded, unable to speak. In his mind he could see the three of them standing there in the snow with their lanterns, ready to come in. She opened the door. Cold white snow blew in out of the darkness, nothing else. Mrs Oldknow stood there smiling at nobody. Tolly flung himself face downwards into one of the big chairs, with angry tears.

'I want to be with them. I want to be with them. Why can't I be with them?' he cried. Mrs Oldknow came to comfort him.

'Don't cry, my dear. You'll find them soon. They're like shy animals. They don't come just at first till they are sure. You mustn't be impatient.' She stopped, then shook him. 'Toseland, listen! Listen! Do you hear what I hear?'

Tolly sat up and strained his ears. Did he? Mrs Oldknow opened the door again, and then he heard it. Faint and muffled by the falling snow a high insistent whinny came from the stables. Tolly listened with bright dry eyes, till the whinny ceased. Toby and Feste were together, and he, Tolly, was content that it should be so.

That night Mrs Oldknow, when she came to see him to bed, stayed longer than usual. The chaffinch was already there, fluffed up in his cage with his head under his wing, taking no notice of either of them. The night-light was lit, and Tolly was pleased to see on the ceiling in the patterned shadow of the cage, the shadow of a bird, as big as a football.

'See how much quicker the shadow-horse goes than the rocking-horse,' said Mrs Oldknow, giving it a forward push. The shadow-horse leaped ahead, stretching out a long neck and forward-pointing ears, as if it could leap out of the room at a bound.

'When I was little, I used to pretend the rocking-horse had got Feste's shadow instead of its own.'

'Who told you about Feste?'

'My grandfather first. But afterwards I used to hear *them* talking.'

Tolly had a very big question troubling him, that could not wait. He wriggled under the bed-clothes until only his eyes showed, and then in his smallest voice he asked: 'Granny, do you see them?'

'Not always,' she said, as if it were quite a simple thing to talk about.

'Did you see them tonight when you opened the door?'

'Yes, darling. They were all three there. At the very beginning I only saw them sometimes in mirrors.'

Tolly came out from under the bed-clothes. 'I do,' he said proudly. 'At least, only Alexander and Linnet, once.'

'Toby is always the rarest. You see, he is often with Feste.'

'Do you ever see Feste?'

'Never,' she said sadly. 'But my grandfather told me he did sometimes.'

Tolly breathed again. There was still hope.

'Was his name Toseland too?'

'Yes, my dear, it was.'

Tolly put the ebony mouse into his pyjama pocket, thinking to himself it would make it come warm more quickly. Mrs Oldknow watched him.

'Is the mouse behaving?'

He grinned happily. 'Not bad,' he said.

In the morning he was woken up by the chaffinch scolding and tut-tutting, and the sound of its feet skidding on the polished floor. At first he thought it must be having a fight with another bird, in the far corner of the room behind some boxes. He got up to look. Outside it was still snowing hard. He could see nothing out of the window but passing flakes.

The chaffinch was tugging at a piece of string that went down between two floor-boards where the crack was rather large. His claws were spread to give him a better hold on the floor, but when he arched his back to pull and jerked his head, his claws slipped again, so that he was clearly cross.

Tolly gently moved him away and lay down to look into the crack. He pulled on the string, but the other end was fast to something. It looked to him like an iron ring. He could not move it however much he pulled or poked. At last he remembered an old silver button-hook that lay at the back of a drawer in the table. (The chaffinch by now had lost interest and was collecting fluff under the bed.) With the button-hook Tolly was able to give a tug on the ring and work it about. It proved to be something quite big, and when at last he was able to pull it out of the crack he saw that it was an old key.

His first thought was the right one. The toy-box! The key fitted and turned. Tolly put his hand to the lid, and then stopped. He would not open it without Mrs Oldknow. Down his narrow winding stairs he went helter-skelter, shouting for her at the top of his voice.

'Come and see what I've found. Come quickly, come and see.'

Mrs Oldknow was getting dressed. She came in a quilted black dressing-gown and without her teeth. She looked so old that Tolly could easily believe she was as old as the house. He would not tell her what he had found till she had panted up the stairs and they were kneeling together before the toy-box.

'Shall we open it now?' she asked.

Tolly nodded and they each put out a hand and lifted the lid.

The box was full. Lying right on the top was a long, narrow, leather case decorated with gold patterns. Mrs Oldknow gave a long 'Oh!', as if for once she was really surprised. 'It's Alexander's flute! Oh Tolly, will you learn to play it?' She took it out of its box where it lay in a velvet slot, put it to her lips and began to play.

In almost no time there was a sound like wind, and outside the windows the air was as full of birds as of snow. Somewhere downstairs a little dog barked, and in his pyjama jacket Tolly was sure the mouse squeaked.

The old lady was trembling with excitement. She laid down the flute. Under the flute-case there were books, which her hands touched one after the other, as if she dared not take them out. Suddenly she shut the lid. 'Come, Tolly, let us go and feed the birds since we have called them. We'll look at the rest after breakfast.'

They hurried to finish their dressing and met again downstairs, both their faces so bright with excitement that for all the difference in their age they were very much alike.

Great flakes of snow blotted out all the distant view. The bushes in the garden were upholstered with fat snow cushions. The yew trees by the house were like huge tattered snow umbrellas. The. branches were weighed down nearly to the ground and shielded it from the snow. Underneath them the birds had gathered to wait for their breakfast, shaking off the snow that had settled on their heads and backs during their flight round the upper windows.

'We'll have a bird party to celebrate finding the flute,' said Mrs Oldknow. 'Yes, I'll butter your hands again, and we will put plates of cake crumbs and grated cheese on the floor.'

When it was ready she opened the door wide. She had the flute in her hand and, as she played, the birds flew in – chaffinches, cole-tits, blue-tits, longtailed-tits, robins, wrens and hedge-sparrows were there immediately. They behaved as if quite at home: Tolly was nearly covered with them. The air was electric with the whirr of wings. The blackbirds stood off by the threshold at first, then one by one, as if in a tournament, they charged in long galloping hops into the room and out again with their loot. Close outside in the branches, the most exciting bird Tolly had ever seen was waiting to pick up what the blackbirds dropped.

'Is that a phoenix?' he asked, pulling Mrs Oldknow's

arm. She still had her lips to the flute. She shook her head.

'Woodpecker,' she said, between two notes.

The little birds were well mannered. They gave the impression of talking and laughing and enjoying themselves very much. Tolly thought it was the gayest party he had ever been to. When everything was eaten the robin sang a little song, perching on top of a picture. The tits explored the room, perching right way up or upside down on chair backs, on curtains, on candlesticks and light shades, showing great curiosity and making little polite remarks. They seemed pleased to stay in out of the snow. The blackbirds fought like border raiders all over the garden for what they had taken away. The woodpecker had flown. Mrs Oldknow was just closing the door to keep out the snow when the starlings arrived, late and noisy as usual.

'I won't have them in the house,' she said, throwing out a plateful of crumbs and shutting the door.

She and Toseland took their breakfast and sat by the fire to eat it. Outside their castle walls all was silence again and falling snow, but inside they laughed to each other as happily as if they were bewitched. When they had finished she gave him his first lesson in playing the flute. It was difficult, but he made some sounds that he thought were lovely.

While she was showing him how to do it, his eyes wandered to the window, and there outside, sitting up in the snow with its ears pricked, was a hare. When Tolly ran to look, with shouts of joy, it lolloped away.

Too late then he began to whisper, 'Toby's hare, Granny, Toby's hare!'

They went upstairs together to see what else was in the box. The chaffinch came too, hopping round hopefully as if there might be something for him inside. The books were very big, bound in leather, the pages spotted with brown marks. There were lots of pictures.

'Ah,' said Mrs Oldknow, 'here's the *Aeneid*. That's the book Alexander has in the picture, that his father brought with him from Germany. And here's *Aesop's Fables*. That's Linnet's. She used to look at it in bed, and laugh! Especially at the Ass in the lion's skin. Here's *Merlin the Sorcerer* and Malory's *Morte d'Arthur*. Those are Toby's, but they all loved them. *The History of Troy*. That's Alexander's again.'

'What's this?' said Tolly, dragging out something like a big dog-collar, except that it was so beautiful, in blue enamelled leather with tiny jewels on it.

'You know what that is. Think! You've often seen it.'

'I know, I know! It's the deer's collar. It belonged to Toby, then. I'll put it on Toby's heap. Couldn't we clean it? It looks almost like a crown. Something for Linnet now – she's only got one book.'

Mrs Oldknow poked into the corner of the box and brought out a small painted wooden figure. Its skirts came down to the ground and there was a large shawl over its head and shoulders so that it was the shape of a round bottle and stood up by itself. The paint was rich and old and nearly worn off.

'It's a box,' she said. 'See if you can open it. The lid's at the bottom.'

The bottom came loose with a loud wooden squeak, and out fell another figure, exactly like the first but painted in different colours and just a little smaller.

'She's got a daughter!' said Tolly, opening the second to reveal a third, and a fourth, and a fifth, and so on, until the last one was shaken out, only as high as a pea. They made a family of ten.

'Those came from Russia, when Captain Oldknow went to the Black Sea. And this box from China,' Mrs Oldknow said, handing him a highly polished black box. Inside it were little jugs and bowls and plates, all cut out of ivory and so paper-thin that they were half transparent. The biggest was not as big as a thimble.

'Yes, yes,' said Tolly, as excited as if he were preparing presents under a Christmas tree. 'These are for Linnet's heap.'

He began to set the plates out as if he were laying the table.

'There are no tea-cups,' he said.

'They weren't invented when Linnet was little, only bowls and mugs. Nor were forks. They all ate with their fingers.'

'Do you mean that if they came to dinner with us they would eat with their fingers? Suppose it was stew?'

'They would sop it up with bread in their fingers.'

'Did you eat with your fingers?' asked Tolly, who could never be sure she was not the old lady in the picture. 'And Toby too?'

'Toby, and his mother and his grandmother and his great-grandmother, all the way back to Adam. But they did it very nicely; you would hardly notice. And they had napkins. Aubrey Oldknow's wife (your great-great-great-great-grandmother) was the first lady in this country to use a fork. It was *very* grand. People were afraid to come to dinner in case they did it wrong. Old gentlemen were very annoyed and said they could not enjoy their food picking away at it with a silver prong. Captain Oldknow never would. He said it was fiddle-faddle.'

She handed Tolly a box of ivory and ebony dominoes.

'You can put them on any of the heaps. They all played with them.'

'I'll put it on Toby's because he is the oldest.'

'And your favourite.'

At the bottom of the box, lying from corner to corner, was a long bundle wrapped round in green cloth. Mrs Oldknow lifted it out and put it on the floor while she unwrapped it. At first they saw a tangle of belts, straps and tassels, and then Tolly gave a great cry.

'It's Toby's sword!'

If Toby had fallen a little from his high place in Tolly's admiration because he ate with his fingers, how high he rose now, when Tolly pulled the real sword out of its scabbard! It had a long, fine blade with an edge on each side. Tolly lunged forward to poke the bed with it. It went in about four inches.

'Stop putting swords through the bed-clothes,' said Mrs Oldknow in an ordinary voice.

'Did Toby use it?' asked Tolly solemnly.

'He never stuck it into anyone, if that is what you mean. But he learnt to fence, and he wore it on Sundays when he went to church with his mother.'

'Why doesn't he want it now?' Mrs Oldknow looked at him with an uneasy wrinkled face. Then she sighed.

'Because he's dead,' she said at last.

Tolly sat dumbfounded, with his big black eyes fixed on her. He must have known of course that the children could not have lived so many centuries without growing old, but he had never thought about it. To him they were so real, so near, they were his own family that he needed more than anything on earth. He felt the world had come to an end.

'Are they all dead?' he said at last.

'They all died together in the Great Plague. The farm bailiff, Boggis, had been to London on business and he brought the infection back with him. Toby and Alexander and Linnet and their mother all died in one day, in a few hours. And little Boggis too. Only poor old grandmother was left, too unhappy to cry.'

Tolly sat cross-legged with his head hanging, trying not to show his face.

Mrs Oldknow got up and walked to the door where she could look down the staircase into what Tolly called the Knight's Hall, as if she were looking for some-one.

'After all,' she said, 'it sounds very sad to say they all

died, but it didn't really make so much difference. I expect the old grandmother soon found out they were still here.'

Tolly was watching something travelling across the floor towards him. It was a marble, a glass one with coloured spirals in the middle. It stopped by his listless fingers. He picked it up. It was warm.

He glanced round the room but saw nothing, except that the dust of which the old box and its contents were full was hanging in the air as if newly disturbed. Then under his eyes the dominoes began of their own accord to stand themselves on end one by one, till they made a long regular curving line, each an inch behind the other. When they were all standing, an unseen finger pushed the last one, which fell over and knocked down the one in front of it. With a soft purr which startled the inquisitive chaffinch up into the air, each domino in turn fell forward till all were lying flat on their white faces, showing a long ribbon of black backs.

Tolly laughed suddenly and loudly. Mrs Oldknow looked round.

'Ah,' she said, smiling, 'their grandmother taught them that game. Wouldn't she be surprised when she saw it happen all by itself? That's Alexander. Linnet never could do it right.'

'Aren't they teases?' said Tolly, quite comforted. 'I'm going to look at their books.'

Mrs Oldknow looked at him with loving approval. 'All right,' she said. 'Dust the books first and then wash your hands. The books are very valuable.' She went away.

Tolly did as she said. 'I'll clean Toby's sword for him afterwards,' he thought, settling himself down with the book of *Aesop's Fables* open on the floor. The print was difficult, but he knew the stories and enjoyed the pictures. After a while, he came to the page that had the Ass in the lion's skin, Linnet's favourite. He bent down to have a closer look, but as he did so two hands were pressed over his eyes from behind and he could feel breathing beside his ear. He put his hands up and felt two very little ones and some curls, soft little cobwebs.

'Linnet!' he said at once, trying to catch hold of the fingers, but they melted away and there was nobody.

'All right,' he said, 'you tease – I can tease too. If you won't let me look at your book, I won't let you look at it either.'

He shut *Aesop* up and sat on it, listening and looking on every side. He heard nothing and saw nothing, but underneath him the book began to move, as if someone were tugging at it. Suddenly he was frightened and jumped up and ran away downstairs to his great-grandmother's reassuring company.

'It did feel horrid,' he thought, to excuse himself as he caught hold of her dress and followed her round. She asked no questions and they sat down together for lunch.

Tolly had almost forgotten the snow, but it was still snowing hard. The garden was getting stranger and stranger. The bushes were just hummocks, little hills in the smooth snow. Even the big yews had lowered their branches to the ground under the weight of it and were getting tied down under the drifts. The snow lay thick round the doors and windows, stopping all draughts, so that the room was warm and rosy with firelight.

'This will be a night for telling stories,' said Mrs Oldknow. Tolly was happy.

'And this afternoon I want to clean Toby's sword,' he said.

They spent the afternoon cleaning it together. Tolly did the blade with paraffin and glass-paper. He was very careful and did not cut himself. Mrs Oldknow did the scabbard, which was covered with velvet. Boggis, coming in out of the snow, very skilfully and lovingly undid the belt and straps.

'I was once a cavalry officer's servant,' he told Tolly. 'These straps want soaking in oil for a week before they are touched.'

'Where shall we put it?' said Mrs Oldknow when the sword was ready, all but the belt which Boggis had taken away. 'We must hang it up somewhere. Would you like it in your room? It would make a lovely shadow at night.' They hung it beside the mirror opposite Tolly's bed.

This was the tale that Mrs Oldknow told him by the fire that evening

The Story of Black Ferdie

A long time ago, when Boggis's grandfather was the gardener here, my grandfather Sir Toseland Oldknow was the owner. He had three grown-up sons who kept many beautiful horses. In particular the youngest, Alexander, my father, had a black mare which was famous as the fastest racer in the country. They thought of nothing but horses and could have done with much more stable room. Nevertheless, as you know, one stall was always left empty.

Now it happened in the year when my grandfather was made a Judge that some gypsy caravans passing through this county camped for a while on a common outside Greatchurch. In one of the caravans lived an old gypsy woman called Petronella and her son, who was called Black Ferdie.

Black Ferdie was tall and slim and very handsome. There was no girl who would say 'No' to him when he smiled. He was without an equal as a horse-breaker or as a rider. He was afraid of no horse on earth, but all horses were afraid of him because he sat them like the Devil, relentlessly. He was famous among the gypsies and the pride of his mother. He was in fact a horse thief.

Black Ferdie soon heard of my father's mare and made up his mind to steal her. He began to watch the house, hiring himself out to farmers as a hedge-cutter in order not to attract attention, and he cut off his long gypsy hair and even washed his face.

There was a girl called Ivy who worked for my grandmother as a linen-maid, and she went every day to hang the washing on the hedge to dry. She was a pretty, good-natured girl who loved to talk and laugh. Black Ferdie knew as soon as he saw her that his work would be easy.

He spoke to her every day, and he was so handsome, so amusing and so flattering that very soon he was her best friend. She could think of nothing else and often brought in the washing before it was dry because she could not wait any longer to see him again. Wet days were an agony to her because she could not go out to him but had to sit darning.

One day Black Ferdie, who called himself Tom,

asked her if there was no place at the Hall for him, because if he could work there he could see her all the time.

'It is true,' she said, 'they want an under-gardener, but everybody who works here is a son or nephew of someone who has always been here. Judge Oldknow would never take you.'

'But they took you just because you were so pretty,' said Black Ferdie.

'No indeed. I am the daughter of Mr Alexander's sergeant who saved his life in the Low Country.'

'Well, my beauty, you only have to say that I am your cousin, who has served in the Navy and now wants to settle down. My name is the same as yours, you know.'

'Is it really?'

'Well, what is yours?'

'Ivy Softly.'

'Just what I said. Mine is Softly too, Tom Softly.'

'Oh, Tom! Isn't that strange? I may call you Tom if you are my cousin. But I never knew I had any.'

'Everyone has cousins they never hear of,' said Black Ferdie, and he told her a wonderful tale about a mutiny in the Far East in which he had saved the captain's life, only afterwards discovering that they were cousins too.

Poor Ivy believed all he told her, though she was not absolutely convinced he was her cousin. It was not difficult to persuade her to ask my grandmother to recommend Tom to the Judge. She thought that if it was not true about his being her cousin, it was only a very little lie, and if he became her husband he would be in the family then if he was not before.

So Black Ferdie became under-gardener. He was exceedingly civil and industrious and made a good impression. As luck would have it, the first job he was given was to weed the cobbled yard. As he knelt there all day, picking out the grass and mosses, he saw the horses being led out and in, and admired the black mare that he had come to steal. He noticed where the stable key was hung.

That evening Judge Oldknow was entertaining one of the neighbouring squires to dinner. While this was in progress, Black Ferdie sat in the kitchen with his arm round Ivy, telling breath-taking stories about the Navy to the other servants.

Most of it was quite impossible, because he had never been to sea, but neither had the other servants, so they believed everything, with the exception of old Boggis, who every now and then gave a most irritating sniff when Tom's conduct (in the story) was more than usually admirable.

When he could hear that the gentlemen in the dining-room were growing merry and noisy, Black Ferdie made an excuse and slipped out into the yard. Stealing round in the shadow of the buildings he entered the stables.

Earlier in the evening he had given young Boggis, who was to watch the horses, a bottle of wine to pass the time away in case the gentlemen drank late. He found him now, as he expected, asleep in the harness-room with his head sunk on the table. The lantern hanging from a nail in the wall only lit a corner of the stable corridor. Outside, the rising moon was hidden from the earth by mist and trees, but high-sailing clouds caught its light and with their silver-gilt brightness reflected a glimmer through the stable windows that was enough for a thief's trained eyes.

Black Ferdie took a bridle and moved quietly along the stalls. Most of the horses were lying down, dim shapes that stirred and blew, shaking their manes. Ferdie passed them one by one, accustoming his eyes to the gloom. The neighbour's horse was standing, being in a strange stable. It was a staid old hack of no interest to him.

The black mare was also standing, because she was a fidget. As she sensed his presence her head flew up as high as the halter would let it, and she snorted and sidled into her corner.

The moon must have cleared the trees, for just then the light grew stronger and Ferdie saw in the stall beyond hers a horse that had not been led past him during the day. He had counted them, and his eye, used to rounding up horses at night, could recognize them more certainly than you or I could by day. This horse was a chestnut with four white feet, with an arch to its neck and a spring in the movement of its haunches, a nervous delicacy in the lifting of its feet that put all thought of the black mare out of Ferdie's head.

'Now, there's a horse for a man to ride!' he thought,

and turned into the chestnut's stall with the bridle in his hand.

As he approached, whistling softly, the horse turned its head towards him, putting back its ears and showing its teeth and the white half-moons of its eyes.

There was no rattling of the halter ring to which it should have been tied. Black Ferdie saw that it was as free and relentless as he was, and that there was a quality of moonlight in its eyes and teeth that his nerves could not endure. He ran in sheer terror, but the horse reared round after him, wheeling through the narrow openings and out at the main door.

It caught him halfway across the cobbled yard, snatching the back of his belted breeches in its teeth. It swung him dreadfully in the air and tossed him away. He crashed on to the cobbles and broke his knee.

The chestnut stood and lifted its head to give a prolonged, penetrating neigh, so that the cheerful gentlemen indoors put down their glasses to listen with white faces. All the other horses then joined in the clamour, stamping and kicking in their stalls.

'Horse thieves!' shouted Alexander, and they snatched up their pistols and ran out.

They found Black Ferdie lying helpless with his broken knee, his teeth chattering and his face grey and damp with sweat. However, he did his best to make up a story.

'The thieves have got away with the chestnut,' he said. 'I saw the stable door open and I came to see if anything was wrong. They were just coming out with the chestnut, two of them, and when I tried to stop them they rode me down. They haven't taken the black mare.'

The Judge and his guests stood by him with their pistols while the two elder sons did what they could to ease his knee. Alexander, with the servants, went to search the stables. The eldest son, while he was trying to arrange the injured man so that he could lie more easily, pulled a pair of pistols out of his great-coat pocket, while Ferdie swore with rage.

'Look, sir,' said the son, 'he was armed!' Alexander came back then.

'Everything's all right, sir,' he reported, 'except that Harry Boggis is asleep beside a bottle of wine. It takes more than a bottle to put him under the table, so I guess it was drugged. One of our bridles was lying in the black mare's stall.'

'Come here, Alexander,' said his father, 'and be a witness to what this man says. Now Tom, which horse was stolen?'

'The chestnut with four white feet,' said Black Ferdie with his teeth chattering. 'In the stall next to the black mare. It rode me down and broke my knee. Hurry, sir, you may overtake them yet. There were two up.'

'The chestnut in the stall next to the black mare,' repeated the Judge.

Nobody spoke, and Ferdie's hair began to stand on end. The Judge's guest, who had not yet spoken, now took a lantern and held it to Tom's face.

'I know this man,' he said. 'He is a gypsy known as

Black Ferdie. He sold me a horse last Michaelmas at Norwich fair.'

'Take him up,' said the Judge, 'and lock him up safely for the night. In the morning we will send him to the prison hospital.'

Poor Ivy cried bitterly when she confessed that she had told a lie about his being her cousin. The Judge would have sent her home in disgrace, but my grandmother pleaded for her, because, she said, Linnet loved her so much. They all thought she meant me – I was only a baby and I had no mother – but sometimes now I wonder.

'What happened to Black Ferdie?'

'He was tried and found guilty and sent to Botany Bay in Australia.'

''What did his old mother do then?'

'No more questions,' said Mrs Oldknow, suddenly in a hurry. 'Old Petronella was as bad as he. Worse. Now off you go to bed.'

There were many things waiting for him in his bedroom now. The chaffinch was curled up and fluffed out on its perch. The not-quite-ordinary mouse was there to be put under his pillow. There were all the quivering shadows thrown by the night-light, and now there was a new one. Behind Toby's sword was another larger, fiercer, man-sized sword hanging on the same nail. The books were on the table. They made mountainous steps on the sloping ceiling.

Tolly took the Russian doll and placed that on the

table too, beside the night-light. At once its shadow stood in the room, nearly as big as St Christopher. There seemed hardly any space left for Tolly himself, so he pushed the doll a little further away from the light till the shadow grew smaller. 'I don't want it any bigger than Linnet,' he thought. 'Linnet wrapped up in a shawl.' When the room was comfortably full of shadow doubles of things he liked, and his own shadow had sat up in bed and stretched a long arm to touch the outstretched nose of the shadow rocking-horse, he blew out the candle by his bed and curled up to sleep.

Outside the wind was singing, and soft noises came from the windows which would have been rattling if they had not been cushioned up with snow. Tolly slept, and his dreams were most wonderful, but when he opened his eyes in the morning he could not remember at all what they had been. The window-panes were covered thickly with frost-patterns of forest ferns – he could not see the real world at all. The chaffinch was pecking at the glass on the inside, but the window was frozen shut.

'Come, chaffie,' said Tolly, holding out a finger. 'I'll let you out downstairs.'

The chaffinch flew to him as if it understood, and they went downstairs together. The other birds were feeding at the open door where Mrs Oldknow stood.

Outside, the world was most magical. It had stopped snowing. The garden looked like the back of a giant swan curled up to sleep. There was nothing but white slopes, white curves, white rounded softnesses with bright blue shadows. Nothing had been scraped aside or trodden on. The only footmarks were the birds' round the door. The yew trees had disappeared. In their place were white hills with folds and creases in their sides. Tolly picked up a handful of snow and found it was made up of tiny violet stars. He could hardly eat his breakfast for excitement.

'Can I go out in it? I won't be able to walk without making marks.'

Mrs Oldknow hesitated. Then she smiled.

'I won't allow Boggis to sweep or walk round here,' she said. 'I love it so much quite untouched. But you have never really met deep snow before. You must learn what it is. You can go, darling. You are just the right age.'

'I won't mess it just here,' he said. 'I'll go round by the wall and keep out of sight.'

He set off, taking huge strides, sinking in to the top of his legs at every step, so that the snow was needle-cold on his bare knees and thighs. St Christopher was a snow-buttress stuck on the side of the house, up to his armpits in a drift. Tolly made slow progress, so slow that with everything unrecognizable it was quite hard to know where he was. He looked backwards and saw his own dragging footprints, like wounds in the snow. In front of him the world was an unbroken dazzling. cloud of crystal stars, except for the moat, which looked like a strip of night that had somehow sinned and had no stars in it. The water was blue-bottle black with slabs of green ice floating just beneath the surface.

Thick snow banks overhung the edge. Tolly could see them at the far side with snow caves underneath, so he was careful to keep away from the near edge lest he should go through.

Where was anything he knew? Was that hump the position of the Green Deer, or was it only an ivy bush? Which of these strange shrouded trees had the green squirrel sitting in the drift against its trunk? And what was that in the pathless garden that looked like a giant snowman eyeless among the slender tree-trunks and the soft hills that might cover anything?

The smell of the snow made him feel a little dizzy, and the deep silence and the absence of any footprints but his own rather frightened him. He felt like turning back and running for home, but who can run when up to his waist in snow? It was then that he noticed some other footprints beside his own.

Along the top of the snow, as if their owner had almost no weight, pointed feet were printed, a little animal that went in long bounds. It had gone towards the snow tent of a yew tree. The footprints disappeared inside the folds of the thick curtain. Tolly followed the trail, feeling ashamed that he could not help leaving such big ugly marks behind him. He bent down to go in under the tree without shaking the snow off the branches. As he crouched at the entrance, he heard the enchanting notes of a flute near at hand.

Inside was a high, tent-shaped room with branches for beams and rafters, lit with a shadowless opal light through the snow walls. In the centre, leaning against

the bole of the tree, were Toby and Alexander, with
Linnet sitting on the dry yew-needle carpet at their
feet. It was Alexander of course who was playing,
while a red squirrel ran up and down him, searching in
his pockets for nuts. Toby was feeding the deer, the
real deer, the beautiful dappled deer with black ears
and a white breast. It wagged its tail like a lamb as it
ate from his hand. Linnet was playing with the lanky
hare, making it stand up and dance to the music. With
its long ears raised it was taller than she as she knelt.
Her little dog danced on its hind legs more vigorously
than the hare to attract her attention.

Tolly was afraid to breathe or move lest they should
vanish, but their eyes were all on him, and they smiled.
He sat down just where he was, by the snow wall, and
said nothing.

All kinds of animals were round the children. There
was a shallow bowl of milk on the ground from which
a hedgehog was drinking. Beside it, a rabbit that had
just finished was sitting up wiping its whiskers. Alexander took the flute from his lips just long enough to say,
'Keep an eye on the fox. I don't want him to hurt the
rabbit.'

Tolly looked round, and there next to him, sitting
up like a dog with the sharpest of sharp looks, was the
fox.

'He's not so bad,' said Toby, 'and he has had a piece
of meat. But he needs watching.'

Up in the branches were hosts of birds. A thrush was
learning the tune. Whenever Alexander stopped, it

tried a solo. Then he would play the notes it wanted and the bird would repeat them. Robins and tits, of course, were everywhere, and field mice running backwards and forwards taking crumbs to their larders. High up in the shadows, looking very haughty, sat the woodpecker. Every now and then it tapped the tree in time to the music but twice as fast. Toby poured some more milk into the bowl. The hedgehog was contentedly moving off, but a mole was putting its nose to the milk.

'That's Truepenny,' said Linnet. 'Poor Truepenny, he's blind. Let me have the squirrel, Alexander. I'm tired of Watt. He's too dreamy.'

'Funny Watt! He reminds me of a poor scholar at Cambridge. He is very intelligent, you know.'

'He's too well-behaved,' said Linnet. 'He's all Sunday-go-to-meeting. He's one of Cromwell's preachies.'

'Nonsense,' said Toby. 'Watt is lovely magic. Haven't you ever seen him dancing with his bride in the twilight? He is cousin to the leprechaun and a distant relation of Feste.'

Just then there was a harsh noise at the door, like a badly cracked bugle, and a silly face wearing a crown was thrust in, followed by a long thin neck that never seemed to end. It closed its eyes and opened its beak to repeat the horrid shriek, advancing to draw behind it a gorgeous body and a tail like a coronation cloak. They all laughed.

'There's your high society for you, Linnet; the confounded peacock. No more music now, nothing but shrieks and posturing. We might just as well go.'

They were gone, like a magic lantern picture when the slide is taken out. A shower of loose snow came down from the branches as all the animals disappeared. Tolly had a feeling as if he had been dropped into the snow out of the sky. He did not know where he had been, nor for how long. He gazed round, noticing again the terrible silence of the snow. There was no sound, his ears ached with silence. After so much life there was suddenly nothing, no one but himself. Then he saw there was one other – Truepenny, who was blind and moved uncertainly. He looked bewildered too. Tolly picked him up. He was soft, velvety and helpless, with pink hands and feet.

'Poor Truepenny! I wonder where you came from? Can you hear flutes from your tunnel under the grass? You'd better go home again – it's all over.'

He put the mole down and waited to see it shuffle away into a heap of dead leaves that perhaps hid its hole. He sat for a while looking at the empty, glimmering, magical tent. Had he been dreaming? When at last he crept out again between the snow curtains, the sun was shining and above the snow the sky was blue. Somewhere in the garden a thrush was trying to whistle Alexander's tune.

Tolly followed his own footsteps now. 'Without them,' he thought, 'I feel as if I could get lost.' On the way, he looked again at the hump that might perhaps be over the Green Deer. It had a slightly rumpled look,

like a bed when someone is pretending never to have
been out of it. Through a thin place in the snow he
recognized the bent brown stem that was the deer's
back leg. Tolly tripped and fell full length in the snow.
He got up and slipped again and the snow went into
his mouth. He began to feel dreadfully tired, as if this
bit of garden had been a great journey.

He was glad when he reached the house. Mrs Oldknow was waiting for him by the door. When she saw
his eyes shining like big lamps she was very gentle.

'Sit down,' she said. 'I'll help you to get rid of some
of this snow. I expect your Wellingtons are quite full.
Pull! And all up inside your sleeves and your trousers –
you are packed in snow!'

Tolly said nothing, but leant against her, and it felt
nice. She was real, certain, and understanding. They ate
their lunch without talking; it was chicken and Tolly
was very hungry so they both enjoyed it. Afterwards
he came and leant up against her again because he
wanted to talk privately.

'Granny,' he said, 'isn't it queer?'

'You've seen them all three, then, today?'

'Yes, under the tree.'

'That's because of the deer. It always goes there
when the snow is deep.' Tolly did not like to mention
the stem leg that he had seen afterwards sticking out of
the snow eiderdown. It puzzled him too much.

'It's a wonderful snow house,' he said. 'It's like being
in heaven and playing in the clouds. And then the
confounded peacock came and spoiled everything.'

'It's the silliest thing that ever lived,' she said. 'And stuck up! Was it wearing its crown?'

'Yes, on its stupid little head.'

'On the end of a long, long neck like a hosepipe.'

'All the better for seeing round corners!' They both began to laugh, as people do when a silly mood takes them.

'It can't decide whether it has hands or feet.'

'When it walks it lifts up its toes like the hands of grand ladies, as if it wore rings and was looking for its handbag.'

'Then it scratches its ear with them.'

'It's deaf. It ought to have an ear-trumpet.'

'Then it and its wife could shriek at each other in turn.'

'What would happen if you trod on its tail?'

'I think it would hiccough.'

When they had finished making sillies of themselves and Mrs Oldknow had wiped the laughter tears from her eyes, she suggested a lesson on the flute. Tolly was willing. 'But,' he said, 'Alexander has got it. How can there be two of it?'

'The one he has now is part of him. This is the one he used to have. It is like a snake-skin when the snake sloughs it off.' Tolly was displeased with this idea.

'No, Granny. This is Alexander's flute. It's the real one. I know it is not a flute-skin.'

He put it to his lips, curling them under in a funny smile as she had taught him. And though it was he who blew and moved his fingers it felt to him as though the stops pulled his fingers to them and the flute took his breath and played itself. A phrase of rippling notes came out. Tolly was ravished.

'That's what Alexander was playing to the birds,' he said.

He put it to his lips again, and the flute played it all through. Mrs Oldknow listened: for once she was completely astonished.

'I think Alexander has given you his flute,' she said. 'I'll teach you all the tunes he played. We will have some music every day, and you shall sing too.'

Before tea Tolly plodded out in Boggis's footsteps to the stable. He looked everywhere for prints of horses' hooves, but he saw none. He left a lump of sugar, being careful that Boggis should not see, for he could not forget Mrs Oldknow's suggestion that it went into the blue tin tea-mug. What could I ever do, he wondered, to make Feste come for me? That of course was his highest ambition, but he almost despaired of it.

After tea there was another story by the fire. 'It is about Linnet this time,' Mrs Oldknow began. 'All the stories cannot be about Feste. It is about the river again, because the river is a very lively inhabitant here, always to be reckoned with, and there are many stories about it.'

Linnet's Story

*I*t was Christmas Eve. There had been snow, then a
dripping thaw that had filled the river, followed by
a sudden hard frost. The trees dangled with icicles that
tinkled like Japanese bells. The eaves were jagged with
ice daggers. The ground was hard like glazed rock, the
moat frozen. Toby and Alexander, with their mother,
had gone on foot to Midnight Mass at the big church
in Penny Soaky across the river. The little church in
this village belonged to what Linnet called the preachies, who did not celebrate Midnight Mass. The family
had gone on foot because the road was too slippery for
horses, the ruts too hard for a coach. Linnet could not

walk so far, so she was put to bed and the grandmother sat downstairs alone. Linnet took Orlando, her little black-and-white curly dog, to bed with her.

She had a little spruce tree in her bedroom – it was her own idea – for the birds. On such a cold night her tame birds had come in to sleep in its branches. They were curled up with their heads under their wings. The tits were balls of blue, or primrose-green; the robins red; the chaffinches pink. Linnet had put a crystal star on top. It glittered among the shadows in the candle-light.

As she lay in bed she heard the wind singing through the icicles outside. It was an eerie sound that made her think of the enormous silence of the country across which it blew. Every now and then an icicle broke off with a sharp crack.

Linnet lay and listened, thinking of her mother and her two brothers walking along the field paths in the brilliant moonlight with their black shadows following under their feet. If she listened for the outside noises she could hear the water going through the water gates and over the weir. The was no flood, but a deep, strong current. She could hear occasionally the owls and the desolate herons. Once she heard a fox bark. Inside her room perhaps one of the birds shifted and chirped softly in its sleep. She could hear Orlando breathing into his own fur. She could hear the candle flame fluttering like a little flag. It was all so very quiet.

Presently she heard something else, something very

strange. Outside on the ice-hard ground there were footsteps that could be nothing and nobody that she knew, not Boggis's hobnailed boots, not her grandmother nor the quick young maid, not a horse! She was not frightened, she was simply certain that it did not belong to the everyday world. Orlando woke up and listened. Linnet could feel his tail softly beating against her ribs.

She got out of bed, wrapping herself in the cover so that she looked like the Russian doll, then she opened the window and leant out. Orlando stood beside her with his paws on the window-sill. She could distinctly hear the steps, heavy but soft, coming along the side of the house. The wind was like a knife against her cheek and all the stars twinkled with cold. Orlando's reassuring tail was wagging against her.

Out into the moonlight came St Christopher himself, huge and gentle and with his head among the stars, taking the stone Child on his shoulders to Midnight Mass. As they went past, Orlando lifted his chin and gave a little cry, and from the stables came a quiet whinny. All the birds in the spruce tree woke up and flew out of the window, circling round St Christopher with excited calls. The stone giant strode across the lawns with his bare feet and soon came to the river. At the edge there was thin, loose ice that shivered like a window-pane as he stepped in. The water rushed round his legs and the reflection of the moon was torn to wet ribbons. The stream crept up to his waist and, as he still went on, to his armpits. When it looked as if he could go no farther Linnet heard a child's voice singing gaily.

The sound was torn and scattered by the wind as the moon's reflection had been by the water, but she recognized the song as it came in snatches.

> Tomorrow shall be my dancing day
> I would my true love did so chance
> To see the legend of my play
> To call my true love to the dance.
> Sing O my love, O my love, my love, my love,
> This have I done for my true love.

As the Child sang, it clutched St Christopher by the hair to hold him firmly.

St Christopher felt his way carefully foot by foot, through the deepest part and came out safely on the other side. Linnet saw him striding away across the meadows. The birds returned, coming in one by one past her head at the open window and chattering as they settled down again on the tree.

When St Christopher was out of sight Linnet realized that it was cold. She also remembered that she had got into bed without saying her prayers. She said them now, and Orlando lay on her feet and kept them warm till she had finished. Then she got into bed again and before long the bells rang out for midnight, and it was Christmas morning. When the boys came back she told them what she had seen. Alexander said he too had seen St Christopher kneeling among the tombstones outside the church in the shadow of a big cypress tree. He thought nobody else had noticed.

Of course they rushed out first thing in the morning to look, and found St Christopher in his place as usual with icicles all over him, but the sun was falling on the stone Child and the hand that it held up looked almost pink.

Tolly went up to bed, taking some crumbs for the chaffinch to eat in the morning. And who knows, perhaps the mouse too. When he reached his room at the top of the stairs, he was delighted to find a pair of tits there as well. 'Perhaps I'll have a Christmas tree with a star on top. That will make another lovely shadow.' There were the two china dogs on the chest of drawers staring him in the face. 'What can I do to have an Orlando? I can't put those icy cold things in my bed. Besides, they might fall out and break. I'll have to make do with the mouse.' When he was in bed he stroked it in his pyjama pocket and said, 'Mouse, mouse, come alive. Mouse, mouse, be magicked.' The mouse gave a twist in his pocket and squeaked, and climbed out and ran across his neck and squeezed past his ear, and flipped his cheek with its tail. But Tolly was already asleep.

The next morning, to Tolly's immense relief, the snow was still lying thick and sparkling, its surface touched only by the light feet of birds. There had been a fresh fall in the night that had half-filled Tolly's steps of the day before, so that they only showed as deep dimples. He could hardly wait to go out – much too anxious, lest he should find no children in the tree house, to be able to eat his breakfast. He stood by the door into the garden and fluted for all the birds and animals to hear, as a sign that he was coming as soon as he could.

He set off after breakfast round the corner past St Christopher, who was still warmly blanketed up by drifts of snow and wore a cowl of snow that wrapped his head and the stone Child's together. He tried to follow his own tracks but soon lost them. The wind had blown the drifts into different shapes. It was a new journey, as lonely and difficult as the last, but this time he knew what he wanted to find. He could see the pyramid of snow that was the yew tree. He would find the opening if he had to struggle through snow up to his neck. All the while he looked right and left for the springing trail of the squirrel, but it was Watt's ears he saw at last, sticking up from behind a hummock. Watt lolloped slowly along as if to show him the way, till Tolly, with his heart thumping with suspense, crawled after him through the low opening.

They were all there. Toby's handsome head was bent over a piece of rope that he was splicing. The deer was munching hay and oats out of a wooden bucket beside him. It looked round as Tolly came in, scratching behind its ear with a hind hoof. Linnet and Alexander were putting Linnet's little gold bracelet round the squirrel's neck. It fitted beautifully. They looked up together, meeting Tolly's eyes as so often in the picture. Tolly had bottled up so many questions inside him that they had to come out.

'Where is your mother?' he said.

'Why, in heaven of course, Ignoranty.' (Linnet said 'Ignoranty' as if it were a pet name.) 'But she doesn't mind our coming here.'

'Was the Great Plague awful?'

Alexander looked up smiling. 'No,' he said. 'It only lasted a few hours. I'd forgotten all about it.'

'I don't remember it at all,' said Linnet. 'What was it, Alexander?'

'Who's Ignoranty now?' said Toby.

'I am. I don't know anything about your stupid Plague,' said Linnet, laughing and rolling over, with her curls all mixed up with yew needles and ivy leaves. It seemed that anything was funny enough to make Linnet laugh. She couldn't help it.

'If you rolled about in the snow outside you would be a Linnet-snow-sausage.'

'Mind the milk! Truepenny hasn't been yet.'

'I did flute for him,' said Tolly, 'in case you hadn't got your flute with you.'

'I've given it to you,' said Alexander.

'Oh, oh! I've rolled on Hedge-prickles!' said Linnet, sitting up and rubbing her arm as the hedgehog hurried away. Orlando came to comfort her.

'Did you make that enormous snowman with no eyes?' Tolly asked Toby. There was a silence.

'Over there, I mean,' said Tolly, pointing through the wall to where he thought it was, 'among the trees, as big as St Christopher.'

'Oh, Ignoranty! He means Green Noah,' said Linnet.

'Keep away from him,' said Toby.

'I'm not afraid of him,' said Linnet. 'He can't hurt me. I'm dead.'

'I didn't mean you, little Flipperty-gibbert – I mean him,' said Toby, nodding towards Tolly.

'Don't go near him,' said Alexander. 'He is eyeless and horrid.'

But Linnet was dancing round Toby in mock solemnity with turns and curtseys.

'I made up a rhyme to tease him,' she said, quite irrepressible. 'I dance round him and I sing, like this:

> Green Noah
> Demon Tree
> Evil Fingers
> Can't catch me!'

Toby made a grab at her, and while they tussled and laughed together Alexander said, 'The only thing the confounded Peacock is good for, is that it always gives warning if Green Noah moves.'

'Where is the Peacock?'

'I expect it's sulking because you and Granny laughed at it so much.'

'Why, where were you when we were laughing?'

'Sitting in the inglenook. Toby was in the other.'

'Yesterday? Why couldn't I see him?'

'Well, you were sitting in the same place, so how could you? It's as if you were both in the same person.'

Tolly sat breaking twigs between his fingers as he

tried to work out this new problem. But it made no sense to him – it was too hard. He looked up again to grin at Alexander, but found he was alone. They had all gone.

Never was a little boy more desolate than Tolly. He wanted them so much, every minute of every day, and he had no sooner found them than they vanished. With hot, salty tears he scattered the heap of broken twigs under his hands, and there lay an old bracelet, bent and black, a tiny one that would fit a squirrel's neck. 'They always leave something where they have been,' he thought, comforted, as he brushed the soil off it. He spent some time trying to get his own narrow hand through it, and at last he succeeded. He plodded back to the house, marching up to Mrs Oldknow with his hands behind his back.

'Guess what I've found.'

Mrs Oldknow took hold of his hands and pulled them to her. He held them out with tightly clenched fists, and she wasted much time trying to open his fingers. At last she felt something under her own fingers round his wrist. She knew at once. Her wrinkles creased up in a boyish, excited smile.

'My own dear little Linnet! You've found her bracelet! Tell me where it was?'

'She put it round the squirrel's neck. It looked marvellous there, all glittery in the fur.'

'She would, of course! I might have thought of that. But she might just as easily have put it on Truepenny, who would have taken it down to wear in the dark of his tunnels. It was a present from her Granny on her sixth birthday. Let's clean it up. Look, she is wearing it in the picture.' They took it in turns to rub it till it was bright gold again.

'Can I have it?' said Mrs Oldknow. 'I know you found it, but I would like to keep it.'

'Yes,' said Tolly, feeling very proud. 'You can keep it. I have the sword.'

'It will have to go to the jeweller's to be mended. Look, the seed-pearls have gone out of these little holes.'

Every few minutes there was a fizz from the fire, as drips came down the wide chimney, but they were too much interested in the bracelet to notice. Afterwards they had a music lesson, in the course of which Tolly called out, 'Granny, look! The snow's all melting.'

It was thawing fast, slipping off the trees in big, slushy drops, and turning to mud on the paths. Tolly could hardly believe that all those powdery drifts could turn wet and nasty and sink away so quickly. By tea-time the tree house had nearly gone. The branches showed through, green and dripping.

'Unless it freezes hard tonight, we shall have another flood,' said Mrs Oldknow. 'If it does freeze, pity the poor birds! Their feet would be frozen on to the branches. We must leave your window open, but not enough for the owls to get in. They snatch little birds while they are asleep. Perhaps the tits and robins will follow the chaffinches in.'

'I've got an idea. May I go and ask Mr Boggis for

something?' Toseland ran out. He found Boggis and asked him to cut some big branches of evergreen, as big as he could. Boggis cut some four-foot lengths of stout ivy, a large branch of bay, and the top of a laurustinus that was like a young tree. All these Tolly carried upstairs to his room. He fixed the branches upright, tying them to the backs of chairs; the ivy he laid along the beams. Then he opened the window, from which he seemed to look down on the sun setting in streaks of grey mist, and took up his flute. 'Help me please, Alexander,' he said, putting his lips to it, and the flute and he played together.

The birds heard. One by one they flew in and inspected their lodging. Two robins quarrelled over a bush, but in the end one of them went to bed in the doll's house instead, where he spent the night in the music room where the beams were just the right size for a perch. Tolly set the window just wide enough to let a late-comer in. He thought an inch and a half would do, but was not quite sure how thin an owl could make itself. Cats, he knew, could squeeze through very narrow gaps. After all this, he went downstairs again, very pleased with himself.

'You haven't ever told me a story about Alexander.'

'Very well, I will tell you one tonight.'

Alexander's Story

All of the children, as you know, because you have heard them, had beautiful voices, but Alexander's was the best. Toby and he sang in the choir in the church in Penny Soaky, where they were very strictly trained. They also sang at home, for their mother played on the spinet and was a clever musician. It was a great treat when their father and elder brother were at home too, to add a bass and a tenor to their part-singing and to teach them sea shanties.

On one of Captain Oldknow's visits he took the whole family to Greatchurch to dine with some friends, and afterwards to see the sights, in particular the church famous for its music and its stained glass. This was at a distance of twelve miles. The Captain and his three sons rode. The two ladies and Linnet went by coach. It was Linnet's birthday. She had a new Dutch doll and was wearing her best dress, the one you know from the picture, and her mother too. In fact the picture was painted not very long afterwards, in honour of the events of which you are going to hear.

At the house of their friends there was much laughter and excitement, first for welcome and pleasure, but also because of the latest news – the proposed visit of the King to a neighbouring mansion. The conversation during dinner was all about it, for it was expected that some kind of entertainment would be provided for His Majesty in the evening, at which all the young people of the county had hopes of appearing, either as performers in the masques, or as members of the audience.

'There is no hope at all for you, my dear,' said Captain Oldknow to Linnet. 'We are quiet country people with no friends at court. No one will think of asking us.'

After dinner they walked to the church to admire the stained-glass windows that had escaped damage from the pikes and stones of Cromwell's soldiers, and so could show to the future the riches that almost everywhere else in the country had been wantonly smashed. The children followed their parents in, expecting to see a church like any other, but bigger and handsomer. It was, however, quite different. It was more like an empty banqueting hall, but so long and so high that, as they stepped inside, they felt themselves dwindle to the size of ninepins. The four walls seemed to be all stained glass, with only enough stone to hold them together, but the stone was decorated high and low with carved crowns, animals and flowers.

Linnet looked round in astonishment. 'Alexander!' she said. 'It's one of Merlin's palaces.'

Alexander could not speak. He was beside himself with delight at the building and the glass.

The afternoon was dull, so that the colours in the windows were deep and rich like sunset seen through a wood, and the stone vaulting looked velvety. A verger was lighting candles two by two all round the walls. Alexander listened to his footfalls sounding like finger-taps on a kettle-drum under the high hollow of the roof. The whole place was vibrating and ecstatic. He felt as if he had fallen under an enchantment, as if he could do impossible things. 'But it's not Merlin's cheating castle,' he thought. 'It's name should be *Joyous Gard*.'

He strayed from his family the better to concentrate on the sensation of tingling emptiness and expectation in the building that he found so strange and so enthralling. If one of the other visitors, intent on looking up at the high windows, made a false step, the sound came to him remote and beautiful as if a pigeon with flapping wings had taken off in the roof. When Alexander was separated by the length of the building from the others, who were just going out by the west door, he heard the final syllable of Toby's voice slipping in a whisper down the wall from the roof at the east end, where he stood himself. It was queer to think of it travelling silently like a butterfly across the immense length of the honey-combed vaulting, to fold its wings and drop there in a half-breath of sound to his ear.

Alexander stayed on, making no sound that could remind them that he was left behind. How could they go so soon? But he was glad to be undisturbed. The verger had gone, and no one else had as yet come in. He stood alone in a magic world. The candles waved in the air that was as much in movement as if in a forest. Every now and then a spindle of wax breaking off a guttering candle fell into the brass holder with a bell-like note that seemed to go up and up and be received into Heaven. Alexander held his breath and listened. There was no sound except a low droning of wind passing along the distant vaulting, the kind of sound that is in a shell.

He had a sudden great desire to sing, to send his voice away up there and hear what nestling echoes it would brush off the roof, how it would be rounded and coloured as it came back. Standing by the choirstalls he sang what first came into his head, part of a new song that his mother was teaching him. He tossed his notes up, like a juggler tossing balls, with careless pleasure. He could feel the building round him alive and trembling with sound.

> I call, I call, I call, (*he sang*)
> Gabriel! Gabriel! Gabriel!

He stopped to listen. It was as if the notes went up like rocket stars, hovered a second and burst into sparklets. The shivered echo multiplied itself by thousands. One would have thought every stone in the building stirred and murmured. He tried it again, louder.

Gabriel! Gabriel! Gabriel!

He could almost imagine the Archangel must hear, might come. He looked round, suddenly awestruck. To his confusion he saw that he was not alone. Leaning out of the organ loft was a Jack-in-the-box of a man with a pointed red beard and a bald head like a marble.

'Boy! Boy!' he shouted, and all the echoes roared like lions. 'Boy! Boy! Stay there (*there*). On your life (*life*).'

Alexander thought he was wild with anger at his presumption in daring to sing. He decided that, considering he was in church, he had better stay and take his scolding.

The little man burst out of the organ-loft stairs, seized him by the arm and held him relentlessly. He had light eyes with very black pupils, like a parrot's, and his beard was raised like a weapon every time he shut his mouth.

'What's your name, boy? Where do you come from? Who is your father? Your father is just outside? Come along, take me to him.'

He dragged Alexander with him, still holding him as if he were a wild animal that might escape.

'There he is, with my mother and my brothers and sister.'

'Sir! Sir! (What did you say your name was, boy? Oldknow?) Captain Oldknow! Sir!'

All this commotion attracted the attention of the passers-by as well as of the Captain whose son was being dragged towards him as if for fearful punishment.

'Oh my dear sir! Dear lady! What a voice, the most astonishing voice! I can't take a refusal. This boy must sing. He must sing before the King. It's a miracle. Calling me by name! Gabriel! Gabriel! (He sang this in a squeaky falsetto). Admit it was startling.'

Captain Oldknow interrupted the stream of words with an amused gesture. 'What is all this about, sir? And why are you dragging my son as if he were a malefactor?'

The wild man clutched Alexander all the more desperately.

'No malefactor, sir an angel. The voice of an angel. I cannot let him go.'

'Alexander,' said his father, 'can you explain all this to me? How did you meet this gentleman?'

'Gabrieli McTavish, at your service, sir,' interrupted the old man.

Alexander, feeling very foolish, explained as best he could, and all his family laughed with him.

'Now, dear sir,' said the Captain, 'I begin to see what this is all about. My son has been experimenting with echoes and has raised one where he least expected it. It seems that his few notes were approved of. Is that all?'

'All, sir! Sir, it falls to me to arrange the musical diversion for His Gracious Majesty next month, but my best boy's voice is breaking. I dare not trust it, and the second best boy is sick. I was in despair, I was like to be disgraced. But now we have only to come to an arrangement.'

The gist of the matter was that the organist, Gabrieli McTavish, was to produce the masque *Cupid and Death* before his Majesty, and by a series of mischances there was no boy available who could sing the part of Cupid. If Alexander were to stay and be trained for the part, all the family could have seats for the show.

'Oh!' gasped Linnet and her mother together, with such feeling that it was probably from a wish to give them pleasure that Captain Oldknow decided to allow Alexander to live with their friends, if they would take him, until the royal visit, and be trained by his new singing master.

On the great night, the Oldknow family coach joined the procession of other more elegant coaches driving to the magnificent house where the King was being entertained. The drive in itself was an extraordinary excitement, for they saw the arrival of all the nobility of the district; and among them the court beauties and their escorts. More amusing to Toby was the running hither and thither of liveried servants with lights; the haughty grooms with handsome horses drawing their empty coaches out of the way and shouting at their rivals when wheels became interlocked or ill-guided horses sidled into theirs.

Seats had been found for Alexander's family in the musician's gallery, from which they had an excellent view of the King's party and the masque. The story that was to be acted and sung was this: Cupid and Death had put up at the same inn, and while they were sleeping, the arrows in their quivers were changed over, so that afterwards whoever was shot by Death, instead of dying, fell in love, while whoever was shot by Cupid, instead of falling in love, died. This was all very amusing, because Death shot the old people, who as lovers were ridiculous; and laughing Cupid was vexed and perplexed when all his young lovers died. On the whole Death had the most fun, but he took it gloomily.

If Alexander was nervous of appearing before such a grand audience he did not show it. He was a wonderfully mischievous Cupid and sang with confidence. His voice was the success of the evening, though Linnet shared his popularity when she hung over the balcony at the close of the play and shouted 'Bravo, Cupid!' in the silence when everyone was waiting for the King to rise.

The King turned to look, and smiled to see Linnet blushing, with her hand clapped over her mouth. He talked awhile with the ladies who were with him, the younger of whom seemed gently to urge him to send one of the gentlemen in waiting on an errand. This gentleman found Alexander in the actors' room and told him that His Majesty did him the honour of sending for him. Alexander followed him through the jostling, staring crowd, feeling very naked, as indeed he was, having nothing on but a wreath of flowers, a white Grecian kilt and his wings and sandals. In front of the royal dais he dropped on to one knee. The King, who had a long sarcastic face and melancholy eyes, looked at him mockingly but with pleasure.

'Take his bow from him,' he said to a gentleman standing near. 'I cannot risk any more trouble. My hands are quite full already. Master Cupid, these ladies desire to know you better. Your arrows may be sham, but your voice, it would seem, strikes home. You have given us and our companions pleasure and we should wish to give you some token of it. In your present nakedness it is impossible to guess what you might lack. Have you any boy's wish that your King might supply?'

'Your Majesty,' said Alexander simply, 'I would like a flute.'

'You shall have it. Addio, Master Cupid. It was well sung.'

So that was how Alexander got his flute.

Mrs Oldknow's fears were justified. It did freeze that night. The air sang with frost as Toseland lay in bed, and the birds roosted in his hospitable branches. The owls hooted outside. Their sound seemed to echo from a glassy, frost-hard sky. Tolly could literally hear how wide the meadows were.

He was dropping off to sleep and already his waking thoughts were mixed with dreams of an echoing palace inhabited by a man with eyes like a parrot, when a direful shriek startled him and he huddled in bed, wide awake. An owl had come close to the window, perching on the gutter with his ogre claws. His voice sounded almost in the room. The birds twittered with fright, the mouse squeaked and so – if truth must be told – did Tolly, pulling the bedclothes up to cover his ears. It was with an effort of courage that he dared to look towards the window to see if the owl could possibly get in. His night-light had guttered out in the draught and he had to strain his eyes for the movement of shadowy forms against the dim window.

There was something outlined against the panes. It was the back of a curly head, and two little fists hammering on the glass inside scared the owl away. He heard a scamper of bare feet, and Linnet's voice saying, 'Ugh! My feet are cold. It's a punishment because I said my prayers in bed tonight. I hope the owl doesn't come back.'

'I'll go next time,' said Tolly.

'*Matthew, Mark, Luke and John, Bless the bed that I lie on,*' said Linnet.

'You're saying them in bed again,' said Alexander.

'I know, but *he's* going to be punished for me next time. He said he would.'

Tolly and Alexander laughed and there was peace and company in the dark room. If the owl came back, they were all asleep.

Next morning there was a fringe of icicles all round the roof, as if the house needed its hair cutting. The trees twinkled with needles of ice. The garden was an ice switchback. At breakfast Mrs Oldknow said: 'I must really get ready for Christmas. There are only a few days left.'

'Can we give *them* a present?' said Tolly.

'What would you suggest?'

'*The first day of Christmas my true love gave to me,*
A partridge in a pear tree.'

Tolly was thinking aloud.

'I think that would be perfect, but a little difficult. Not absolutely impossible. It would be difficult to get a live partridge and harder to make it stay in the tree. It ought really to be a tame one.'

'It could be in a cage, and we could tame it afterwards.'

'I'm sure they never had a partridge. Linnet would love it, with all its brood running after it like tortoiseshell thimbles with legs. Let's try, Tolly. It's a perfect idea. We'll advertise: 'Wanted, live hen partridge, preferably tame.' And I'll write to a gamekeeper I know in Scotland. Bring me my writing paper, I'll do it at once.'

Tolly and she enjoyed themselves writing what seemed ridiculous letters. They also chose out of a catalogue a pear tree described as having 'juicy melting flesh, delicious flavour'.

While they were writing, Boggis brought in some magazines and a note from a neighbour, who offered to drive Mrs Oldknow in to Greatchurch if she had anything to do there, and also to take her to a concert.

'That means I can't take you, Tolly. What a shame. But we will go together another time. Boggis will have to look after you. Please thank her, Boggis, and say I will be ready at eleven. What are those papers?'

'Something about the house, ma'am, that she thought might interest you.'

Mrs Oldknow with her baskets for the Christmas shopping went off in her friend's car. Tolly went out into the garden. The snow, first melted and then frozen over, looked messy, lifeless and uninviting. There was thin ice on the moat, not strong enough to bear his weight. He went to the fish platform and broke the ice there, clearing a pool and throwing bread in. Neptune's ugly snout with whiskers made of flesh like sea-anemones came and sucked it in. But Tolly could not love Neptune. Mrs Oldknow said that when he was young he was almost as pretty as a goldfish. Tolly fed him for Toby's sake, but thought he was horrid.

Turning away from the pool he looked around for the tree that during the snow had been like a snowman, the tree called Green Noah. He was startled to find himself so near it. In the tangle of briars, saplings and brushwood which the wood path, that he had so often followed, skirted at a careful distance, stood a tall yew column, roughly shaped like Noah with his usual square shoulders and fantastic flat bowler hat. It was not surprising that Tolly had not noticed it before, because it was so long since it had been trimmed that it had grown wild and hairy, its outline almost lost. Most shocking of all, two long, undisciplined arms had grown out from shoulder height with open fingers and hanging sleeves. Tolly was seized with panic and ran as fast as he could over the icy slopes to find Boggis.

Boggis was whitewashing the little saddle-room where he kept his blue tea-pot and mug and his primus stove. Today he had a little fire in the grate. His face looked redder and his eyes bluer than ever, and the whitewash had a comforting, homely smell.

'Can't do nothing outside today,' he said. 'I made a fire so we could have our dinner cosy-like, seeing that you're alone.'

At each side of the grate old horse-shoes were hanging, arranged in overlapping rows to make a sort of frame for it. They were all different, as if one had been kept from each horse that had lived there. Boggis had whitewashed the wall and had hung them all back on their nails. Tolly studied them with interest. How they varied! Some were obviously cart-horses' and some ponies', but in between were the carriage horses' and the hunters', the thoroughbreds'. One perhaps was Feste's. Is there among horse-shoes one that stands out for its delicate curve, suggesting the perfect hoof, the sure and dancing step? Tolly thought so. He chose out one shoe for his love, and when Boggis was not looking he wrote in the clean circle of wall behind it, 'Feste'.

'Boggis,' he asked presently, 'have you got a grandson?'

'I had, but he was killed in the last war.'

'Well, have you got a son?'

'I had, two. But they were killed in the first war.'

Tolly was upset by this news. How would anything go on if there wasn't a Boggis? Then he remembered that he was only there himself as if it were sideways, through his mother.

'Well, haven't you a grand-daughter, then?'

'Yes, I have. And she's got a son.'

'But he won't be called Boggis.'

'Yes, he will that.'

'Oh, then that's all right.'

'No, it isn't all right. It's all wrong, because she isn't married.'

'But there must be a Boggis, mustn't there?'

'Well, Master Toseland, I shouldn't say so, least of all to you, but I do like to think he'll have the name. The child just missed being called Liquorice, and what sort of a name is that!' Boggis guffawed, rocking on his heels. 'Percy Liquorice! That's what he'd have been. And his mother's a good girl barring accidents.'

Boggis spread newspapers on the table for a cloth and sent Tolly to fill the kettle and to fetch the sandwiches that Mrs Oldknow had put ready for him. They sat down one each side of the blue tea-pot. Boggis hung his cap on the point of a horse-shoe. His bald scalp was as white as a hard-boiled egg above his scarlet face. He made the tea, taking the tea-leaves from his waistcoat pocket. The sugar was in the pocket on the other side. He slipped the spoon straight into it. So it was unlikely he had taken the lump sugar put out for Feste.

Tolly thought his own sandwiches were so much nicer that it was embarrassing. His were ham, and then cheese and lettuce, and afterwards banana. Boggis had slabs of bread and mustard-coloured pickle. He refused any exchange with scorn.

'I like something you can taste,' he said. 'These pickled onions eat lovely.'

'Did you know my grandfather?' said Tolly as they munched.

'That I did. He was a limb of mischief, he and his brothers. There were six of them. I remember one day they were all in that field at the back here, looking for mushrooms. The bull had been put out with the cows and the boys hadn't noticed, till all of a sudden he was well-nigh snorting in their pants. I seed them all run for the river and pop in one after the other, swimming with all their clothes on like so many frogs. I couldn't help but laugh. My son was batman to your grandfather in the first war. They were killed together. In the second war it was my grandson as was the sergeant and your father was his corporal. He carried my grandson across an open bridge when his legs were shot off. That's how he came here and met your mother, Miss Linnet. He came to see me and bring my grandson's things and tell us about him.'

'Tell me about my mother.'

'She was a proper caution too. Many a time she made me laugh, she did say such things. I remember once when she was only a little thing she said to me, "Boggis," she said, "are you as red all over as your face is?" She did! Are you as red all over as your face! "No, Miss Linnet." I said, "I'm as white all over as my head is," and I pulled my cap off to show her. How I did laugh!'

Boggis's tales were not nearly as good as Mrs Oldknow's. The queer thing was, that the nearer to the present time they were, the more remote they seemed. Tolly was far more interested in Toby than he was in his father as the corporal.

After lunch he wandered back to the house. It seemed very empty without Mrs Oldknow, as though not only she had gone, but all the possibilities of the house had gone with her. Even the picture looked different, and Tolly was almost surprised to see that the children's grandmother was still there.

On the table lay the two magazines that had been brought in by Boggis. Tolly looked at them. One was called *Here and There*. There was a red pencil mark under the title 'Homes the Crusaders Left Behind Them'. It was a long article, too full of historic references for Tolly to read, but it was illustrated with photographs of such houses as still existed from which crusaders were known to have gone. Green Knowe was one of them, and there was a photograph of St Christopher and an imaginary drawing of the Chapel.

The other magazine was called *Adam's Seed*. It was

all about gardening, and the sender had marked with red pencil 'Some Unusual Topiary'. There were photographs of different things that had been cut out of yew and holly – yew eagles, a yew ship, yew chessmen, crowns, armchairs, a holly horse, a yew lady in a bath in a willow summerhouse plaited like a basket out of living wands. Turning the page he came upon the Green Deer, the squirrel, the hare, the cock and hen – and Green Noah, a photograph taken a long time ago, because it showed Noah smaller and closely trimmed. Tolly began to read in earnest.

'Perhaps the most unusual and romantic of these examples is that of the Green Noah which now gives its name to the estate on which it stands, though the original name was Green Knowe. The story about it is widespread. It has been told me in much the same form in different 'locals' all over the county, and also still further afield, by old men who remembered hearing it in their childhood. It seems that an old gardener called Boggis first shaped the various animals and later added a figure of Noah. He was much addicted to drink and suffered from delusions, but no one can deny his skill, and his employer appears to have allowed him a free hand. When Noah was a few years old and growing nicely, it happened that a famous horse thief was caught red-handed in the stables of Green Knowe, as it was still called. He came up before the owner, Judge Oldknow, for trial. He was condemned, and after lying in Newgate prison for some years, he was deported to Botany Bay. His mother, Old Petronella, a gypsy and a notorious witch, is said to have revenged herself by breaking into the gardens during an eclipse of the moon and there with horrible dancing and laughter that was heard in the house (though no one knew what it was that so chilled their blood) she laid a curse on the Green Noah. The traditional version is:

> Snippet snappet
> Shapen yew
> Devil's image
> Take on you.
>
> Evil grow,
> Evil be,
> Green Noah
> Demon Tree.

'As the tree grew, a series of unexplained accidents overtook the men of the family, in every case due to shying or bolting horses. According to the villagers, the horses panicked because of a blind figure that prowled by night. Some say that Old Petronella herself was caught by him in the end. Before long the name Green Knowe was forgotten, the people insisting on calling it Green Noah. The photograph that is reproduced here is at least thirty years old, as for a long time nobody has been willing to trim the Old Gentleman. It is to be hoped that in the end he will lose all resemblance and the curse will lapse.'

As Tolly finished reading the story, he suddenly

realized that not only was Mrs Oldknow still away, but Boggis had finished his work and gone home. It was nearly dark, and he was alone. For some reason he felt convinced that until his great-grandmother returned, not so much as a marble would move in the house. He felt no such assurance about the garden. He lit all the candles, made up the fire, laid out the tea, and sat down to wait in the inglenook where once Toby had sat. He played sad little tunes on his flute with many wrong notes, and he wished with all his heart that she would come back.

When at last he heard a car he hurried to meet her.

'I thought you were never coming!' he said.

Mrs Oldknow had masses of parcels and was laughing with pleasure. 'Tolly, my dear, I've had a lovely day. I've brought back the Christmas tree – Boggis has taken it into the stables. And I've done some lucky shopping. Let's have tea at once and I'll tell you all about it. Oh, darling, you've put everything ready!'

She seemed as pleased to be with him again as he was to be with her. They laughed as they ate: they found everything funny. They made silly remarks for the sake of laughing at them. She told him about an old friend whom she had met for lunch who had grown a little queer in the head. 'She wore two hats and two wrist-watches, neither of which would go: but she knows a lot of sporting people. And I *believe* I've got a partridge. I must ring up an address she gave me tonight. If it's all right we'll go together and choose a pear tree at the nursery gardens. The old nurseryman

who has sold me garden things all his life will think I
have gone mad at last, when I say I want a four-year-
old pear tree and it must have branches strong enough
to bear a partridge cage and partridge. You say it,
Toby. It won't matter so much if you seem mad.'

'You called me Toby,' said Tolly, putting his arms
round her neck from behind.

'Well, how can I tell which of you it is when you
are behind me?'

'Well, it's Tolly, unless Toby's in the same place as
me, like Alexander said.'

'Well, if it's Tolly, you can tell me what you did all
day.'

'I had a picnic with Boggis. He keeps his tea in one
waistcoat pocket and his sugar in the other. He just
puts the spoon straight in.'

'Very convenient. My Boggis had an old tail-coat
with pockets in the tails. He had a bottle of beer in
each and he kept his sandwiches in his hat.'

'Boggis's were horrible yellow ones.'

'Pickled onions, I expect, like his grandfather's. They
would taste better with beer than with tea, but Boggis's
grandfather drank so much beer that it has frightened
his descendants ever since. They have all been tee-
totallers.'

There was a silence.

'And what else, my dear?'

Tolly noticed, when they were not talking, that the
silence now had not that dead and frightening quality
that it had when Mrs Oldknow was away. He could

not quite say whether he heard or only felt, that the house was alive. Perhaps it was only the wind, but there seemed to be movement. A great deal was going on out of sight. He turned, comforted, to his great-grandmother.

'And what else, my dear?' she repeated.

'These,' said Tolly, handing her the magazines *Here and There* and *Adam's Seed*. 'I read these.'

Mrs Oldknow turned over the pages and soon came to the story of Green Noah. She read it quickly while Tolly watched her face.

'Yes,' she said, 'that's the end of the story of Black Ferdie. I didn't want to tell you lest you should be frightened. But we leave Green Noah alone and take no notice of him. He is growing into quite an ordinary tree. The curse is very old and I suppose it doesn't last forever. Old Petronella and Black Ferdie died ages ago, and they don't care any more.'

'I only saw it this morning. I never noticed it before, it's so wild and uncut. Only it made a snowman.'

'I know.'

'I thought it hadn't eyes because no one could reach to put cinders in.' Tolly couldn't help a shudder.

'Don't think about him. St Christopher is much more lasting.'

'Linnet's not afraid of anything,' said Tolly, whose thoughts moved quickly from St Christopher to Linnet and from Linnet to the owl. Perhaps Mrs Oldknow's thoughts went the same way.

'How were the birds last night?' she asked.

'They made an *awful* mess. Don't they know?'

'It is surprising from such well-mannered little things. They don't know and they can't learn! You'll have to spread newspapers. It thawed this afternoon, but it is freezing again now. How the owls screamed last night!'

Tolly laughed, partly because he had been so frightened, partly with pleasure because the little birds had been safe. 'I hope they screamed with rage,' he said boldly.

They went upstairs together. As they entered Tolly's room there was a sound of rustling leaves. The birds were there already. The candles made tree shadows covering all the others. Mrs Oldknow tucked him up and said good night, and very soon he was asleep.

He dreamed that he was sleeping in the doll's house with Toby, Alexander and Linnet in the three other beds. Toby was telling them all a wonderful story. Tolly could not have said what it was about, but it was wonderful – when suddenly he broke off with 'Hush! Keep silent!' and cupped his hands round the nightlight to cover the light. Tolly heard shuffling, leafy steps as something came into the real bedroom, fumbling round as if it were dark, though the night-light was burning. Tolly in his doll's-house bed could see everything. The Thing found its way to his own empty bed and suddenly pounced on it. It gave a silent yell like a gale in a tree, and threw the bedclothes right and left. Then it went fumbling round the room, feeling in the corners and on the saddle of the rocking-horse, but it never thought of the doll's house. At last Tolly saw that it had turned into an owl. It stood in the middle of the room doing a kind of war dance, lifting first one claw and then the other and swaying its head. Its shadow was huge. Then Toby got out of his bed in the doll's house and took his night-light and set it under the owl's tail feathers. There was a loud spluttering and commotion. Tolly woke up to find an unfortunate moth in the wax of the night-light. He was in his own bed.

One or two birds shifted and called as if in their sleep. Had they been dreaming of owls too? He thought he could hear gentle breathing in the room, and then suddenly, as if it had only just begun after being asleep itself, the slow tick-tock of the clock came to his ears, almost as loud as a hammer.

The next day Mrs Oldknow and Tolly set out by bus to visit the nurseries where they were to choose the pear tree. Tolly's mind had been busy. He had notions of his own about a present for his great-grandmother, an idea that had come when he was turning over the pages of *Adam's Seed*. It suited him very well to go to the nursery garden.

They were met by the old foreman. He looked like a field-mouse, if a field-mouse could be as big as a small man and wear an old grey hat and gaiters. His eyes twinkled and his movements were quick and sudden. Mrs Oldknow could never get to the end of a sentence before he answered, 'Yeslady', or 'Nolady', as the case might be, speaking rapidly as if he were nibbling. Tolly thought it was a pity he had no whiskers to wiggle as he said it. He said 'Yessir, Nosir' to Tolly who had never been called Sir before. While Mrs Oldknow was wandering up and down the lines of young pear trees to pick a strong one, Tolly put a private question.

'Have you a rose in a tiny pot that only grows three inches high?'

'Yessir. Rosa minimissimasir. Threeandsixpencesir.'

'Does it smell?'

'Yessir, they saysosir; if your noseissmallenoughsir.'

Tolly had some money which his father had sent him, so he paid and put the tiny parcel in his pocket. Then he joined Mrs Oldknow. The pear tree was a little disappointing because of course it had no leaves.

'The one in the illustration to the song was in full blossom, not just sticks. I suppose they did it by magic,' said Tolly sadly.

'Mustavedonesir, suresir,' said the foreman.

It was thawing slowly, but they spent the rest of the day in the town, where they forgot all about the snow which, in any case, had been shovelled up there and carted away. When they came home again at tea-time it was to find the garden green and brown and sodden.

Tolly's thoughts were full of Christmas, for there were now only three days to go. He received a letter from Burma, from his father. The envelope and stamps were exciting, but the letter made him feel further away than ever. There was a P.S. in an oversized scrawly writing: 'Mother sends love to Toto.' Toseland put the letter in the fire but kept the envelope.

At night he dreamt of Christmas. He found the field-mouse foreman decorating the Christmas tree. This time he had long wiggling whiskers. He was busy hanging up coconuts, and strings of peanuts, pears hung on skewers and bags of silver net full of almonds and raisins. His eyes were brimming with twinkle and his cheek was full of nuts. He hung up a small round red cheese. Presently, out of his bulging pockets from which hung a tail of raffia, he pulled a parcel wrapped in paper on which were printed coloured maps. It was covered all over with foreign postmarks. He looked at this, wiggled his whiskers, and dropped it at Tolly's feet.

Tolly unwrapped it, as full of anticipation as if he expected Aladdin's lamp. Inside, in cotton wool, were two plastic big toes such as you might buy from the joke counter in toy-shops to fit over your socks. There was also a card saying 'For little Toe-Toe'.

Tolly was in a rage. He stamped and shook the Christmas tree furiously. The field-mouse foreman stopped, staring at him, and suddenly with frightened eyes dwindled to a real field-mouse and, with his tail held up, whisked away and disappeared.

Tolly woke up quietly. 'Mouse?' he said into his pillow, and thought he felt a wriggle under it. He laughed softly to himself. At breakfast, grinning over the top of his cup at Mrs Oldknow, he said, 'I've thought of a present for Boggis.'

'Clever boy. Boggis is always so difficult. What is it?'

'Two plastic big toes to fit over his socks to frighten his wife with!'

'Where have you seen those?'

'I haven't. I invented them last night in bed. But somebody else may have invented them too. Conjurors have pretend thumbs with long iron nails sticking through them to frighten people. Who decorates the Christmas tree?'

'You and I do. We'll do it tomorrow.'

'Shall we hang presents for the birds – I mean coconuts, peanuts and things?'

'We will, outside on the yew tree for Christmas Day. And hazel-nuts for the squirrels and woodpecker. And biscuits on the ground for the robins and blackbirds.'

'I dreamt all that,' said Tolly proudly.

'You're a good dreamer. What else?'

'Well, there's Truepenny and Hedge-prickles, and there ought to be an invitation to field-mice.'

'Truepenny and Hedge-prickles could have some truffles for a great treat. I've a little jar that was given me that I don't think I shall ever use. And field-mice love bird-seed. You shall make trails from different parts of the garden, leading to the tree.'

'It will be *their* tree, of course.'

'Of course! Which else? You wouldn't want to hang everything on Green Noah to make a Christmas tree of him, would you?'

Tolly only grinned. He was in high spirits and had

more grins than he knew what to do with. So much so, that when he was larking round the garden by himself, not looking for the others but just taking it for granted they were there, he had a sudden inspiration to show off for their benefit. Dancing along the path that circled Green Noah, which was as near as he could come because of the brambles, he chanted Linnet's song at the top of his voice.

> Green Noah
> Demon Tree!
> Evil fingers
> Can't catch me!

Then he did a kind of war dance, such as the owl had done in his dream. He was so pleased with it that he capered off across the lawn, getting wilder and wilder, stamping, whirling and pointing till he bumped into Boggis.

'Anyone would think you had been drinking, acting so silly,' said Boggis severely. 'Mrs Oldknow is waiting for you to decorate the tree in the music room.'

Off ran Tolly, still full of joy.

'We must do it today,' said Mrs Oldknow. 'There will be so much to do tomorrow – look, Boggis has brought in the holly and the ivy and the mistletoe. We will put that up first.'

When they had finished decorating it, the old room looked more like the Knight's Hall than ever. Against the stone walls, on top of the stone chimney-piece, the dark green leaves themselves looked mediaeval. It was an ancient castle prepared for an ancient feast. When Tolly was handing up great bunches to Mrs Oldknow on the steps, it often seemed to him not so heavy as he expected, as if someone were helping him. 'Did *they* do this?' he asked.

'Yes, they always decorated the house, but they didn't have a Christmas tree. Christmas trees began much later, in England at any rate. They had their feast in our dining-room, which their father had altered and improved. It was he who had our big fireplace put in, and the big windows on to the garden. And it was their mother who first used this as a music room. She used to teach them some of the songs that I teach you.'

It was late afternoon before they finished the Christmas tree, and it was growing dark. They lit the old red Chinese lantern and many candles so that they could see to work. There were no glaring electric bulbs on this tree. Mrs Oldknow had boxes of coloured glass ornaments, each wrapped separately in tissue paper and put carefully away from year to year. Some were very old and precious indeed. There were glass balls, stars, fir-cones, acorns and bells in all colours and all sizes. There were also silver medallions of angels. Of course the most beautiful star was fixed at the very top, with gold and silver suns and stars beneath and around it. Each glass treasure, as light as an eggshell and as brittle, was hung on a loop of black cotton that had to be coaxed over the prickly fingers of the tree. Tolly took them carefully out of their tissue paper and Mrs Old-

know hung them up. The tiny glass bell-clappers tinkled when a branch was touched. When it was all
finished, there were no lights on the tree itself, but the
candles in the room were reflected in each glass bauble
on it, and seemed in those soft deep colours to be
shining from an immense distance away, as if the tree
were a cloudy night sky full of stars. They sat down
together to look at their work. Tolly thought it so
beautiful he could say nothing, he could hardly believe
his eyes.

As they rested there, tired and dreamy and content,
he thought he heard the rocking-horse gently moving,
but the sound came from Mrs Oldknow's room, which
opened out of the music room. A woman's voice
began to sing very softly a cradle song that Tolly had
learnt and dearly loved:

> Lully Lulla, Thou little tiny child
> By by, Lully Lullay.
> O sisters too, how may we do
> For to preserve this day
> This poor youngling
> For whom we sing
> By by, Lully Lullay.

'Who is it?' he whispered.

'It's the grandmother rocking the cradle,' said Mrs
Oldknow, and her eyes were full of tears.

'Why are you crying, Granny? It's lovely.'

'It is lovely, only it is such a long time ago. I don't

know why that should be sad, but it sometimes seems so.'

The singing began again.

'Granny,' whispered Tolly again with his arm through hers, 'whose cradle is it? Linnet is as big as I am.'

'My darling, this voice is much older than that. I hardly know whose it is. I heard it once before at Christmas.'

It was queer to hear the baby's sleepy whimper only in the next room, now, and so long ago. 'Come, we'll sing it too,' said Mrs Oldknow, going to the spinet. She played, but it was Tolly who sang alone, while, four hundred years ago, a baby went to sleep.

They went down then for their tea, which they needed badly, for they had worked long and hard, as well as hearing strange things. Tolly was very good at lighting candles. He did not spill wax or drop red-hot matches. He helped to get the tea ready and made excellent toast. He could hardly believe he was the same boy who had spent miserable holidays alone in an empty school.

'I shall take you to Midnight Mass tomorrow, if you would like to come – and if the weather is possible. It is a long walk. Do you know, I thought I heard thunder a minute ago? Who ever heard of thunder at Christmas?'

Tolly was far too excited to think of going to bed. His head was in a whirl, thinking of the Christmas tree, of the live partridge that should arrive tomorrow, of his present for his great-grandmother, of the probability that there would be some sort of a present for him, of the cradle song in Mrs Oldknow's room, of the children, of the loveliness of everything. The only thing he never thought of was something he had done himself that morning. Now he was trying to contrive ways of staying up longer. Asking questions seemed the easiest way.

'Shall we go to Midnight Mass if it snows?'

'I believe it is thunder,' said Mrs Oldknow. 'Open the door, Tolly, and listen.' Tolly opened the door into the garden. It was a dark evening with tattered clouds in front of a slatey sky. He heard no thunder. It was even unnaturally quiet. Perhaps it only seemed unnatural because he himself was brimming with excitement. He heard the weir pounding at the end of the garden. It only made the quietness quieter. It was rather like a heart that is only heard when it beats too loud. Tolly wondered how loud Feste's heart would sound if you put your head against his ribs after a gallop.

'Granny,' he said, 'I haven't put any sugar for Feste. Can I take the flashlight and go out with some before I go to bed?'

'Yes,' she said. 'Your name should be Hopeful. Shut the door, it's cold.'

He let the heavy curtain fall behind him and went out, shutting the door. He was surprised to see how short were the stretches of garden that the flashlight lit up in front, and it lit nothing at all at the side. It was difficult to find the familiar paths, but he was childish enough to play that he was on a motor bicycle. Instead of going the nearest way to the stable he set off along the lawn, following his tiny beam, intending to go all round the garden side of the stables and in at the far corner. He had just discovered that whichever way he turned it, the beam lit up nothing at all but grass, so that he was not even sure of his direction, when he was startled nearly out of his skin by a long-drawn screech from the peacock. For a minute he thought it was a terrifying bugle. Tolly stood stock-still.

Then came thunder like a rattle of drums. The effect was like the opening of a Punch and Judy show on a monstrous scale, a Punch and Judy show that wasn't for fun. He looked all round. There were no stars. For once the curtains were all drawn in the house and no lights shone. He could see the point of the roof against a patch of sky, but the walls were muffled with darkness, as if it were something real that he would have to struggle through to get back. The garden was not pitch-black, but it seemed covered over with a mass of shadow. There were so many overlapping shadows that he couldn't tell what anything was. He couldn't tell a tree wasn't a shadow till he bumped his face on a branch.

He was alone, and the garden seemed no longer his. He felt like a trespasser as he moved along it. The thought reminded him of Black Ferdie. He wished he had gone straight to Feste's protective stall. His flashlight was growing weaker and weaker. It was only a little pin of light. He shook it. It died out altogether. At that moment he remembered what he had done in the morning. He remembered how he had danced and pointed, and pulled faces. He heard again Toby's voice saying, 'Don't go near him,' and Alexander's saying, 'He is eyeless and horrid,' and 'the only thing the confounded peacock is good for . . .'

The peacock gave a screech that seemed unending. Tolly could imagine how it would stretch out its neck, long and thin, in the effort, with curved open beak and wagging tongue. When it stopped, there was a sound of dragging, of brushing and snapping twigs. The other birds woke and flew out of their roosting places with a panicky twittering. In the dark Tolly could hear them moving from tree to tree across the garden in agitated bands, as if they were escaping from a forest fire.

He himself remained rooted to the ground. He did not know which way to run, where there would not be entangling branches or the edge of a path to trip him up. How could one hide from the blind? They would not even know you were hiding. The fumbling fingers were just as likely to hit on you behind a bush as in the open.

Then there came a flash of lightning in which the whole scene was clearer than the sharpest thought. By its terrible flicker Tolly saw in the middle of the lawn a tree where no tree should be – a tree shaped roughly like a stooping man, that waved its arms before it and clutched the air with its long fingers. In the clap of thunder which followed, Tolly, frozen with terror, raised his thin child's voice in screams of 'Linnet! Linnet!'

Perhaps he had no need to call, for as the thunder died away in distant precipices of sky, Linnet's voice like an anxious bird was beating the air, calling: 'St Christopher, St Christopher, come quickly, St Christopher!'

Other voices joined hers, Toby's and Alexander's, piercing and boyish, and other unknown children's.

Suddenly their cries ceased. Did that mean it was already too late, that in the darkness any moment he would be pounced upon and feel the tightening of the leafy fingers? Or had St Christopher heard? Was he already stirring the creepers and moving out from the house?

Moaning winds were rushing and leaping round the circle of the garden, leaving a silence in the centre where something dreadful was certainly taking place. It felt like the pressure of opposing thunderstorms before they break. The air was prickly and the suspense so great that Tolly could not breathe, could hardly stand, his heart nearly choked him. At last a great forked lightning zig-zagged out of the sky, so bright that Tolly could not see anything else, with instantaneous thunder crashing and rolling, enough for ten lightnings. The air was full of a smell of burning.

'Ah!' said Linnet, Toby and Alexander from the shadows.

'Ah!' said lots of other happy voices. 'Green Noah's gone.'

As Tolly reached the house, not knowing if he walked or ran, the door opened with a flood of warm light and Mrs Oldknow came out to look for him.

'Tolly, Tolly! Are you all right? What's happened? Has anything been struck?'

'Green Noah's gone,' said Tolly, falling in a dead faint in her arms.

'Shall I carry him in, ma'am?' said Boggis, appearing with his lantern. 'I came up to see if you were all right.'

He carried Tolly in and laid him in a big armchair. Then he fetched a jug of cold water and Mrs Oldknow splashed some on Tolly's face.

'He's had a fright, that's what it is,' said Boggis. 'A rare fright by the look of it. I'll go out and see if I can find anything burning, or anyone about. You'll be all right till I come back.'

When Tolly opened his eyes again, the first person they rested on was Toby, who was standing with Alexander by the fireplace.

'Feste's calling you,' said Tolly faintly.

'I know,' said Toby. 'He trumpeted his loudest when old Noah was struck. I was just waiting for you to come to yourself again. I'll go now.'

'I wish I could see Feste,' said Tolly, turning a tired head on his cushion. Toby gave him his most brilliant smile.

'Perhaps Christmas Day is your lucky day,' he said.

'You should try wearing his clothes,' said Alexander.

Linnet and Mrs Oldknow were kneeling by the arm

of his chair. He smiled happily at them; then he remembered how silly he had been and his smile went crooked and funny. Linnet pulled what she thought was a terrifying face and wiggled her fingers at him, and they both laughed. Toby went out, passing Boggis in the doorway, who came in without appearing to see him, or Alexander or Linnet. Tolly was sitting up looking nearly himself again, but Boggis was looking very queer.

'Sit down, Boggis,' said Mrs Oldknow. 'You look upset. What is the matter? I hope there's nothing serious?'

Boggis wiped his bald head with a coloured handkerchief. 'There's nothing burning now,' he said with an effort at calmness, 'but there's been a tree struck. There's a charred stump lying on the edge of the lawn – can't think where it fell from. And there's things moving.'

'What things, Boggis?'

'I wouldn't like to say, ma'am. Things as didn't ought to.'

'Stone things,' said Linnet in a whisper to Tolly, laughing all over her face.

Mrs Oldknow poured out a brandy and gave it to Boggis. 'Drink that,' she said. 'I know you are a teetotaller, but it will do you good. Tolly's had some.'

Boggis poured it down his throat and smacked his lips.

'And I saw something queer too,' he said, beginning to twinkle again. 'I met someone in the garden, and who do you think it was? Now who do you think?' Mrs Oldknow and Tolly made no suggestions.

'Well, believe it or not, if I could believe my own eyes I'd say it was my grandfather Boggis as died sixty years ago. And as drunk he was! – as drunk as a lord and singing hymns to God Almighty!'

This time it was Mrs Oldknow who laughed. Tolly turned to share the joke with Alexander and Linnet, but they had vanished.

'Dear old grandfather Boggis,' said Mrs Oldknow. 'I liked him very much when I was a child. He was so funny when he was drunk! I was never frightened of him. So he's celebrating tonight, is he?'

Soon Tolly was comfortably tucked up in bed and felt at peace with everything. Old Noah was gone for good and all. It even seemed almost a pity.

'What shall we do now?' he asked Mrs Oldknow. 'Will you change the name of the house back to Green Knowe?'

'No, I've come to like Green Noah better. We'll plant a new one. We will have Noah and Mrs Noah, one each side of the flood-gate, and I'll get Father Patrick to come and bless them.'

Next morning Tolly helped Boggis to clear away what was left of Green Noah. He was sawn up and split and taken into the house for firewood. 'We'll burn it on Christmas Day,' said Mrs Oldknow.

'I'd be scared to do it,' said Boggis. 'Too much like hell-fire for me! Might burn the house down with his last breath.'

'I think his last breath has been singed out of him. There's no sap in the wood at all.'

When old Noah was neatly stacked in short logs in the corner of the fireplace, there was the pear tree to plant. Tolly wanted it somewhere near St Christopher. They planted it in front of one of the old chapel windows in the wall, because Mrs Oldknow said she would like to see the children's faces poking through the blossom when it came into flower. 'It always was a hide-and-seek window,' she said.

The delivery van arrived, and there was much secrecy and winking and running to and fro on the part of Boggis, but a basket had arrived labelled 'Live Birds. URGENT', which so excited Tolly that he noticed nothing else. It was found to contain two partridges, a cock and a hen, neat plump little creatures of great charm but rather nervous. Tied to the basket was a card that said: 'I have sent a mate with her in case there are none in your district.' As there were two, they were put in a large coop at the foot of the tree. Tolly fed them and gave them water. He thought they were pretty and funny beyond belief and he was very proud of his present.

Before tea, when it was getting dark, he tied a label on the coop, on which he had printed as well as he could in different coloured crayons:

T   A   L

with much love

from

T

Then he covered the coop with a sack to keep the partridges warm for the night.

When Boggis came in to wish them good night and a Merry Christmas tomorrow, Mrs Oldknow and Tolly gave him a bulky parcel for his great-grandson Percy.

'What are you giving him, Boggis?' said Tolly.

Boggis's face was just a red, teasing twinkle.

'I always give him the same every year,' he said. 'A box of Liquorice Allsorts.'

'Boggis!' said Mrs Oldknow.

'Oh, he likes that, ma'am. He knows it's coming. He looks forward to that.'

Tolly did the animals' tree last of all. Mrs Oldknow had given him several triangles of cheese that he pierced with a wire and hung up on a branch. He had burnt holes in the coconut with a red-hot poker, and that was hung up too. He put the nuts and almonds and raisins in a hollow in the trunk; a mound of crumbs and grated cheese on the ground; another of ants' eggs and another of pine-kernels; the truffles in a saucer near the pile of twigs where once Truepenny had disappeared; a big cabbage for the rabbit and Watt; and some oats in a wooden bucket. Then he laid trails of bird-seed from the four corners of the garden to the yew tree, scattered very sparingly so that the field-mice could not have had enough before they got as far as the party.

That night there was neither thunder nor snow, but a bright moon and keen frost. Before starting to walk to Midnight Mass with Mrs Oldknow, Tolly had been privately to look at St Christopher. The moon shone full on his weathered stone face. He looked as if he had not moved since the beginning of time. As they set off with their moon shadows playing on the path round their feet, Tolly wondered if Linnet was looking out of the top window.

His shadow had long legs that he was rather proud of.

'Granny,' he said, 'your shadow looks just like a partridge.'

'I've often thought you don't always know whose shadow comes out with you.'

They were going to the church where Toby and Alexander had sung in the choir, where St Christopher had knelt unseen among the cypresses and tombstones.

The footpath went along beside the river, through wide flat meadows. It was surrounded by miles and miles of silent moonlight. There was almost no view but sky. Tolly had not yet been to the church; he imagined it as the most beautiful and exciting end to a thrilling walk. In fact he was confusing it in his mind with that other church where Alexander had experimented with echoes and which he had called JOYOUS GARD. In the moonlight the frozen meadows looked like sheets of frosted glass and the river like gold, old gold full of black creases like Linnet's bracelet when they were cleaning it. The cold made an eerie humming in the telegraph wires, a sound that grew suddenly alarmingly loud if Tolly put his ear against the post. There were no lights showing from any cottage window, nor any living creature out in the countryside but themselves. It was a long walk: it took them an hour and felt like a pilgrimage, but they saw nobody else going the same way. Tolly began to feel that he and his great-grandmother were going secretly to meet Toby and Alexander and perhaps their father and mother; that it was to be a mysterious and delightful family affair.

When they came inside the church, the first impression that he received was the mixed smell of incense and clammy mould, with the mould predominating. There were a few other people there, dingy, unromantic townsfolk, no children at all. The church was battered and dank, festooned with cobwebs round the windows, carpeted like a kitchen with brown coconut matting and bleakly lit with electric light. It is true that on the altar there were candles and chrysanthemums, but he could not help feeling that it was ugly and disappointing. There was a huge picture hanging on the wall on his left that was so horrifying that he kept one hand up to the side of his face like a blinker in case he should see it by accident. When they stood up to sing, the organ wheezed out as if it were the funeral march for a cat. Tolly was afraid to hear his own voice above the faint caterwauling that dragged after it. He was tired and felt suddenly very sad. Finally he fell asleep against Mrs Oldknow's shoulder.

When he opened his eyes, the electric light was out and far more candles were burning. The church looked new. The stone, instead of being grey, stained with black damp, was a nice sandy colour. The pews had gone. The pillars rose out of the floor like tree-trunks, leaving the nave spacious and gay. Instead of the wheezy organ there was a sound of fiddles and trumpets. People came in walking freely as if to a party, and stood in groups here and there.

Tolly turned round at a clinking sound close behind him, and there was Toby walking in with his mother on his arm. He was wearing his sword. When he had placed his mother near Mrs Oldknow he bowed formally to them and went out again. His place was taken by someone who could only be a Boggis, who stood respectfully just behind young Mrs Oldknow. She smiled at the old lady and at Tolly, raising one eyebrow at him as if to say, 'You here too?'

When at last he could take his eyes off her and look towards the choir, the boys were just coming in. There were six of them in surplices with white frills round their necks. Two little boys came first. One was laughing and turned to look at them as he went by. Alexander and a stranger came next, and then Toby and another, and after them the men. But Tolly was looking at the first little boy who just could not be solemn, for he knew now that it was Linnet, dressed in boy's clothes, in church, in the choir. He looked anxiously at Mrs Oldknow, fearing to see a look of angry shame come over her face, but she was looking at her book and smiling. He nudged his great-grandmother but she only laid her fingers on her lips and put her hand through his arm.

The singing was beautiful. Tolly knew it was part-singing, but he could only hear all four notes when there was a pause and they all hung together on the air. It gave him pleasure almost painful. Sometimes Toby sang solo for a few minutes and sometimes Alexander. His voice flew up to the roof as easily as a bird. Tolly feared it would make him cry, but that passed off when he saw Linnet hitching up her trousers. They were probably Alexander's and too big for her.

Then, gazing round the church, he saw, or thought he saw, through the wavering candle shadows, leaning against the wall, as much a part of it and as little noticed as if he were at home, St Christopher himself. Linnet was almost opposite him. She made signs that Tolly did not understand until he craned up to see better. Then he saw, pressed against the stone ripples that washed St Christopher's feet, the little black-and-white dog Orlando, fixing obedient eyes on his mistress and thumping the floor with his tail. Tolly gave a little squeak of laughter, but it was luckily drowned in the peal of bells that broke out.

Mrs Oldknow said: 'Wake up, Tolly. A Happy Christmas to you! We are going back in my friend's car, so you will soon be in bed. Did you have nice dreams?'

Tolly looked quite bewildered. 'Yes, Granny,' he said. 'Were you asleep too?'

'Perhaps,' she said. 'I hardly know.'

Tolly slept all the way home and must have put

himself to bed sleep-walking, for he remembered nothing about it. The first thing that he knew was that he was awake in his bed and that it was Christmas morning. The room was still half dark, but right in front of his eyes something was hanging from the bottom of the bird-cage. This was his stocking, with a right-angled corner sticking out at the calf and an elongated toe. The chaffinch was already out, hanging on to the stocking and tugging at the label. It followed Tolly back to bed, and when he had lit the candle they unpacked the stocking together.

There was a flashlight refill from Boggis. A telescope from his father. In his bedroom he could only use the wrong end but it was almost better. He looked at the rocking-horse and it would have fitted into a matchbox. He found Toby's sword, the right size for a chaffinch. The chaffinch was hard to find, no bigger than a ladybird. In the looking-glass opposite his bed he saw himself as if across a wide valley, miles and miles away. And if the things in the room were small, their doubles in the doll's house had reached vanishing point.

The thing that stuck out of the calf of the stocking was a tin box shaped like Noah's Ark, filled with biscuits, each of which was glazed with brown sugar and had on it a picture of an animal in white sugar. He found a hare, a squirrel, a fox, a deer, a dog, a hedgehog, a peacock, a fish, an owl and, of course, a horse. Tolly couldn't bear to eat any of them except the owl. He bit its head off in one bite, then held it out in his lips to the chaffinch, who pecked at it once or twice, then gave a sharp, determined tug and flew away with the piece.

After that they shared the fish, and then the peacock.

Next came two boxes of Bengal matches, one green and one red. Tolly struck one, and saw the chaffinch cock a startled eye like a bright round emerald.

'Now I'll make you see red,' said Tolly, striking a red one.

But the chaffinch did not like that at all. He drew all his feathers tight round him in a fright and flew off to the cage.

The toe of the stocking had a banana, a tangerine and an apple. Last of all Tolly opened an envelope tied to the top. He expected – for no one can help expecting a little – that it would contain a postal order, perhaps for two-and-six or even five shillings. It contained a Christmas card with a picture of two curly white china dogs with black faces. Underneath was written in his great-grandmother's hand:

> Their names are
> Wait   and   See

Tolly laughed, but he felt sure it meant something more. He put his legs out of bed to start to get dressed, but at first he could not see his clothes. Someone had thrown what looked like an old curtain over them. Tolly snatched it off and was about to throw it on the floor when he stopped at the sight of silver buttons all down one side. The stuff was green silk, faded yellow in some places and stained black in others. He held it at arm's length, turning it about to see what it was. It was not a woman's blouse. It was some kind of coat with big skirt pockets outlined in tarnished cord. Tolly put it on and looked at himself in the mirror. His own black eyes looked straight back at him and immediately he knew what he was wearing. His heart felt as if it would jump out of his mouth. 'You should try wearing his clothes,' Alexander had said.

The coat was much too big for him, but he rolled up the sleeves, dropped the apple from his stocking into the deep pocket, and off in his bare feet he went, down the twisting wooden stairs that, with practice, had come to seem so easy and rapid, along the cold brick floor of the entrance hall, running as fast as he could across the hurting gravel drive, hardly noticing the strange morning twilight, only pausing outside the stable. Here he took a long breath and walked with what he hoped was Toby's step into the shadowy stall, closing his eyes for fear of disappointment.

There was a steaminess and a friendly, lived-in smell. Tolly stood there like someone in a trance, with his hands over his face, and heard a stirring of feet in straw, then warm, velvety lips began to try to pull his fingers away from his eyes. With his eyes still closed he put his arms round a bending neck, just behind the ears, twining his fingers in the long mane that fell over them. Then he felt a prod on his thigh from the apple in his pocket, which was being nosed and pushed about. Tolly pushed the apple upwards from the bottom till he heard Feste's teeth crunch into it. 'Oh, why didn't I bring sugar?' he thought. 'Now he won't know who puts it there.' Just then the outer stable door swung wide open with a bang as Boggis tramped in wheeling his bicycle, whistling loudly. The dust raised by the slam must have gone into Tolly's nose. He sneezed and sneezed and sneezed again.

'Struth!' said Boggis, looking over into the empty stall where Tolly cut a peculiar figure in his old-fashioned ragged coat and bare feet, sneezing in the dust of centuries. 'What in heaven's name is going on here? I thought you were a gypsy. What's that you've got on?'

'Happy Christmas, Boggis,' said Tolly. 'These are my special Christmas clothes.'

He went pattering off towards the house, but skirted round the garden path, partly to avoid the painful gravel, partly because in imagination he was riding a high-spirited horse and needed room to gallop. As he came along the lawn he saw the children grouped near the tree. Linnet was holding one of the partridges in her lap and feeding the other with corn. The peacock was sharing it, looking for once very beautiful and gracious. Toby was coatless, wearing a shirt which had full sleeves like a bishop's with lace at the wrist. He looked slim and athletic, as if he had just come from a fencing lesson. He was holding and examining something which, as Tolly drew nearer, stuffing his hands into the pockets of Toby's coat with quiet swagger, he saw was Truepenny. The deer and Watt were browsing at Toby's heels. Alexander was standing by with a handful of nuts which he was cracking between his teeth and eating. The squirrel was on his sleeve helping itself out of his palm.

Toby looked up and smiled at Tolly, raising one eyebrow just as his mother had done in church. 'Come here, Linnet,' he was saying. 'Will you hold Truepenny for me? Alexander's too busy eating the squirrel's nuts. Hold him upside down. I want to get a thorn out of his hand.' Linnet took the little velvet thing and held him carefully. He looked pathetic with his pink palms and soles kicking at the four corners of his body, for his limbs were so short he looked as if he had none. He opened and shut his mouth but no sound came. There was truffle on the end of his nose. One of Linnet's curls, falling forward as she bent her head, lay on his stomach like an eiderdown. Toby had neat skilful fingers and the thorn was soon out.

'Give him to me,' said Alexander. 'I'll put him back among the thruffles.' He said it with difficulty because his mouth was full of nutshell.

'Did they all come?' asked Tolly.

'Oh yes, it has been a splendid breakfast party. I wondered where you were,' said Toby, grinning at him. 'I had to tie Reynard up because the new partridges were too much for him. Even the badger came today. He ate all the raisins.'

Linnet looked round, all alive with fun. 'The partridges are sweet,' she said. 'I've got a pocket full of field-mice, too. Look!'

She put her hand into the pocket of her silk apron

and brought out a bright-eyed handful. One of them she put on the ground. It ran towards Tolly, so he picked it up and tied it in his handkerchief and put it in his pocket.

'I think I'll keep that one and tame it,' he said. They all laughed.

'Yes, keep it and tame it,' echoed Linnet, laughing like a little mad thing.

Her laughter was drowned in a rushing sound almost like a passing aeroplane, but it was only the arrival of the starlings. They descended in a gabbling cloud, blotting out everything else for a moment, and when they had alighted, the ground was carpeted with their waddling shiny figures, pecking at top speed to right and left among the crumbs of the feast. They had the place to themselves.

Tolly had gained a new confidence, perhaps because he was wearing Toby's coat. He no longer feared that the children would disappear and leave him, and perhaps never come back. He felt that they were like brothers and sisters who come and go, but there is no need for worry: they are sure to come home again. He remembered with remorse that he had not yet wished his great-grandmother a Happy Christmas. She was preparing breakfast and smiled when she saw him.

'Good morning, Barefeet. Happy Christmas!' she said. 'Do you like your toes blue with cold?'

'Do you know who I am this time?'

'Why, Toby, of course! That means you will want two eggs for breakfast. Dear me, that coat *is* getting shabby. It is worse than shabby – it is coming to pieces like tissue paper.'

'I'll take it off carefully and fold it up and put it in a drawer by itself,' said Tolly.

'I forgot to tell you,' she called after him, 'Percy Boggis always comes for Christmas Day. He'll be here for breakfast. He's a nice boy.'

When Tolly came back he was properly dressed and carried a very small parcel in his hand.

'It's for you,' he said, 'for when you used to play with the doll's house. It's ALIVE.'

'What good ideas you have!' she said as she un-wrapped the tiny rose tree. 'I always wished so much that there could be such a thing. I never guessed I should ever really have one.'

'It's alive,' he said again. 'It will have leaves no bigger than bird-seed, and flowers like tiny wild straw-berries. It will make a doll's-house room smell of roses.'

'Thank you very much for a perfect present. I will water it with my fountain pen filler, and put a salt-spoonful of compost on it in the spring. As for my present to you, you must Wait and See. I think I hear Percy.'

She went out into the hall to meet him, where there was some whispering before she brought him in.

He was a tough little boy with a shining, apple-cheeked face and hardy blue eyes. When Tolly shyly said 'Hullo', he made no reply, but stared around him like a lion. Mrs Oldknow made them sit down and gave them two eggs each.

'I expect you've both been awake since dawn,' she said. 'How did the breakfast party go off under the tree, Tolly?'

'I think everything is eaten up and everybody came. Hedge-prickles squeaked and grunted when he ate the truffles. He liked them very much. The peacock was quite nice to the partridges, like Miss Spudd with new boys. I brought one of the mice to tame. It's here in my pocket. I'll show you.'

He felt in his pocket while the other two watched him, but all he could find was his handkerchief with something hard in it. He brought it out to see what it could be and put it on the table. It was his own ebony mouse. Percy gave a loud country guffaw, and Tolly felt as if he had unwillingly done a conjuring trick. After a minute he began to laugh too, and so did Mrs Oldknow.

'It won't be hard to tame,' said Percy, and that was his only remark during the meal. He ate a great deal and looked quite at home.

Tolly sat, as usual, opposite the family portrait. He looked from the children to Percy and from Percy to the children again. Percy was so real. You couldn't imagine him vanishing. Tolly felt sure Linnet would have liked him. There ought, he thought, to have been a Boggis somewhere in the picture, if only in the garden that you can see through the window at the back. Or perhaps he was standing beside the painter, watching how he did it, and it was someone like Percy that Linnet was really laughing at, and with; not the artist at all.

Breakfast was over. Tolly's eyes, still smiling from what he imagined in the picture, came down and met Percy Boggis's bold blue gaze, and was answered with a wide grin.

'I went to the circus,' said Percy briefly, as he left the table. 'They did this.'

He did two back-hand springs in quick succession and stood up panting and flushed, and hiccoughed. 'Too soon after breakfast,' he said, and did two forward ones, remaining on the same square of carpet. Tolly stood lost in wonder and ambition to do the same.

'Bravo, Percy!' said Mrs Oldknow. 'I see how you and Tolly are going to spend the day. But wait a moment. We have something to do first. You know what.'

'Aw, aye,' said Percy, disappearing from the room without more explanation.

'Tolly, shut your eyes and hold out both your arms. Come in, Percy. You can give it to him.'

Tolly stood there with his eyes shut, remembering the soft nose in the stables and the bump of the apple against his thigh, when suddenly his waiting arms were weighed down by a bundle of electrical activity so twisting and squirming that it was all he could do to hold it.

'It's Orlando!' he called out, opening his eyes. 'It's a real Orlando! Is he mine?'

'He's yours from now on.' Orlando was tugging at Tolly's sleeve, showing a great deal of white of eye. Tolly could not so much as speak to anyone else without getting his fingers nipped with pin teeth to recall his wandering attention. Puppy barks in a voice not yet broken made all conversation impossible. The two boys and Orlando left off all their surplus energy for half an hour. Then Percy said, 'In the circus they made them jump through hoops.'

'I know where there's a hoop,' said Tolly, 'hanging on a nail in Boggis's wood loft.'

'My old hoop!' said Mrs Oldknow. 'Tolly, your eyes really do see everything. Go off both of you and get it.'

Percy went down the garden in a series of cartwheels. Tolly was learning too, but Orlando was always barking either at his hands or his feet; and if he fell, the penalty was to be nibbled alive with pin teeth down the back of his neck and under his chin, or worst of all, on the bare back of his knees.

There is no need to describe the rest of Christmas Day – the turkey stuffed with chestnuts, the plum pudding that Tolly lit and Percy carried to the table in a circle of forget-me-not blue flames; the crystallized fruits, the crackers after tea, from which Mrs Oldknow drew a white paper bonnet that made her look more like the grandmother in the picture than ever. Tolly and Percy were luckier; their crackers dropped tiny metal aeroplanes and Snakes' Eggs.

Orlando shared everything. He even pulled a cracker with Tolly. Out of it he got a rolled-up paper tongue that, when Tolly blew, shot out suddenly to a stiff arm's length and flipped him on the nose, always slipping back into its roll before he could bite it.

When at last Mrs Oldknow came up to say good night, Tolly and Orlando were quite worn out. Orlando, curled up on the bed, would not open an eye however much Tolly nudged him. Tolly's eyes wandered sleepily over his room, acknowleding all his treasures, and their shadows that he loved perhaps almost more.

'Must I go to school next term?' he asked.

Mrs Oldknow kissed him good night.

'I can't waste your singing on Miss Spudd any more,' she said. 'You are going to the choir school at Greatchurch. I think they may let you sing in the choir. How Alexander would have envied you! And of course all your holidays will be here.

'And your father has written that he wants you to learn to ride.'

AFTERWORD

It can be quite difficult, when you are reading a story, to work out which parts are made up by the author, and which parts are real. An author can put real things and imagined things together in a story, like putting eggs and flour in a cake, and mix them up so well that you really can't sort them out afterwards. In the book which you have just read, for example, you might easily think that the wonderful, powerfully · ancient house, Green Noah, or Green Knowe, with its Norman rooms, and its attic bedroom full of lovely old toys, with the gently creaking rocking-horse, and the window looking out on to the river was something imagined. The more you read about the house, the garden all round it, the creatures clipped into shape from growing trees, the more imagined you might think it was, because after all, it is a very unusual house, almost impossibly old, and impossibly beautiful – the sort of house you might dream about.

Lucy Boston certainly did dream about the house, but she also lived in it, because it is a real house as well as a made up one. It isn't called Green Knowe, it is the Manor House at Hemingford Grey near Cambridge. Lucy bought the house in 1937, and she and her son Peter, with a lot of help from local builders, and some unhelp from experts in old houses, found bricked-up fireplaces, and old windows, that had been filled in and plastered over, and working over two years they put the house back to shape again – one of the many shapes it had been in over the long years in which it had stood beside the river. Then Lucy turned the rough field in which the house stood when she bought it into a beautiful garden. Then she turned the house and garden into books for you to read, of which this one is the first. There are eight altogether.

What about the children of Green Knowe, then? Were they real? The obvious answer is that Lucy, like Tolly, made them up to keep her company in her house. Ghost children must be imaginary. But its hard to be sure of that when you are in the house, or the garden, because it is so exactly like the house in the books that you can't help expecting to hear Linnet's laughter, or see a marble roll across the floor all by itself. And if it did, what would you think? Would you think, 'What a sloping floor this old house has!' Or would you think that Toby or Alexander or Linnet were playing a game with you?

Speaking of her writing, Lucy said, 'All my water is drawn from one well.' The well for her imagination was her house, which appears in all but one of her books. She also told us something which she hoped her books would do for her readers: 'I would like to remind adults of joy, now obsolete, and I would like to encourage children to use and trust their senses for themselves at first hand – their ears, eyes and noses, their fingers and soles of their feet, their skins and their breathing, their muscular joy and rhythms and heart-

beats, their instinctive loves and pity and awe of the unknown . . .'

The story you have just read is full of passages in
which Tolly is using his ears and eyes and nose, and the
soles of his feet, and you are invited to feel and see and
breathe with him. You don't have to be in Green
Knowe to do that – you could use your senses wherever you are in the world.

You don't *have to* visit the real house, when you can
visit the imaginary one just by reading. But you *could*
visit the real house – Lucy died a little while ago, but
her son Peter and his family still live in the house, and
it is open to anyone who would like to visit it, and
who makes a telephone call to arrange it first. Lucy
loved to invite people in, and show them the garden
first, and then the house. She specially liked to show
the house to children who had read some or all of the
books, because it was such fun for them, and for her,
when they recognized things they had read about in
one of the stories.

There's a paradox about Lucy's house; so many
people have read the Green Knowe books now that
you might find the made up things in the story – the
ghost children, for example – seem just as real as the
stones of the house, or the water in the quiet river.
Certainly anyone who has read the books, and then
visits the house sees, not only a very old house with
interesting windows, rather like a church, and curious
rooms, they see Green Knowe, an imaginary house. If
you were visiting the house, you might see, or feel, a

ghost. You might imagine you could see Mrs Old-know, who is, you must have guessed, very much as Lucy Boston was herself.

Jill Paton Walsh